— A *Felicity* MYSTERY —

TRAITOR IN WILLIAMSBURG

by Elizabeth McDavid Jones

Questions or comments? Call 1-800-845-0005, visit our Web site
at **americangirl.com**, or write to Customer Service, American Girl,
8400 Fairway Place, Middleton, WI 53562-0497.

Printed in China
08 09 10 11 12 13 LEO 12 11 10 9 8 7 6 5 4 3 2

PICTURE CREDITS
The following individuals and organizations have generously
given permission to reprint illustrations contained in "Looking Back":
pp. 172–173—Williamsburg street, The Colonial Williamsburg
Foundation; *Miss Juliana Willoughby,* George Romney, National
Gallery of Art, Washington, D.C., Andrew W. Mellon Collection
1937.1.104.(c) NGA; pp. 174–175—battle scene, painting by Don Troiani,
www.historicalartprints.com; The First Continental Congress, 1774.
Allyn Cox, Oil on Canvas. Courtesy of the Architect of the Capitol,
Washington, D.C.; spinning wheel, North Wind Picture Archives;
Williamsburg store, The Colonial Williamsburg Foundation; pp. 176–177—
ship, © National Maritime Museum, London; newspaper clipping,
North Wind Picture Archives; Loyalist being tarred and feathered, courtesy of
the John Carter Brown Library at Brown University; pp. 178–179—Loyalists
leaving for Canada, etching by Howard Pyle for *Harper's Weekly*; print shop,
The Colonial Williamsburg Foundation; *Virginia Gazette* masthead,
Library of Virginia; raising the flag, North Wind Picture Archives.

Illustrations by Jean-Paul Tibbles

Cataloging-in-Publication Data
available from the Library of Congress.

In memory of
Lance Corporal Jason Scott Daniel,
a brave Marine who served
his country well

TABLE OF CONTENTS

1

A DANGEROUS FAVOR

"It's still there, Elizabeth! It's still there!"

On this bright and sparkly spring day in 1776, the door to Widow Reed's print shop was propped open to the morning breeze, and the *clang-clang* of the huge printing press drifted outside, where Felicity Merriman stood gazing into the window, calling to her friend Elizabeth.

Every day for the last week Felicity and her best friend, Elizabeth Cole, had found a reason to walk past Widow Reed's shop just so that they could stare at the display in her many-paned window. Today was such a brilliant spring morning, with the air still crisp but the sun warm, that Felicity couldn't help running ahead of Elizabeth. The girls had just come

1

from their lessons at Miss Manderly's house.

"Come on, Elizabeth," Felicity had called as soon as they were past Miss Manderly's white picket fence. "I'll race you to Widow Reed's!" Off the two of them had sprinted, down Duke of Gloucester Street and around the corner to Widow Reed's painted sign: a town crier holding up a gilded newspaper.

Felicity was all out of breath and her red hair was poking out every which way from under her hat, as it often did, but she was wearing a grin as broad as Williamsburg's dusty streets. It *was* still there—the book that Felicity dreamed of owning for her very own: a beautiful leather-bound copy of *Gulliver's Travels.*

When Elizabeth caught up with her, Felicity happily pointed out the book, displayed prominently among various public notices and samples of Widow Reed's work. "It's still there, Elizabeth. Nobody's bought it yet."

Elizabeth's cheeks were red from running, but somehow *her* blonde hair had managed to stay neatly in place under her cap. "Oh,

2

Felicity," she said, "wouldn't it be grand to own such a book? Imagine having a book all your own!"

Felicity sighed. "I suppose there's no use hoping, though. The price is likely too dear."

"Your birthday's only a few weeks away," Elizabeth said. Felicity's birthday was on April twenty-first. "Perhaps your parents would get the book for you as a gift."

Before Felicity could answer, the girls heard Widow Reed inside the shop, shouting to her apprentices above the clamor of the printing press. "Puller, let's get those sheets onto the press! And, Beater, could you move a little faster with the ink? We've a newspaper to get out today, my boys!"

"Sounds like Widow Reed is hard at work," Elizabeth said.

"Well," Felicity replied, "being the only woman printer in Williamsburg can't be easy. And Father says she's the best. He much prefers her *Gazette* to the two other newspapers in town, because hers has the most news of—"

Felicity stopped herself. "Of the Patriots" was what she had been about to say. But she didn't want to hurt Elizabeth's feelings. Even though the American colonies were at war with England, Elizabeth's family was still loyal to the king. Last winter, Elizabeth's father had been jailed because he was a Loyalist. Felicity's grandfather had helped Mr. Cole get out of jail, but Mr. Cole had had to promise to leave the colony. He'd gone to New York to live, leaving his wife and daughters behind to take care of their property.

"News of what, Felicity?" Elizabeth asked brightly.

"Of the most interest to the most people," Felicity finished quickly. "And speaking of the *Gazette,* I need to go in and get one for Father. I promised to bring it to him at the store."

Her father's store was Felicity's favorite place in all the world, and she knew Elizabeth loved it, too. It was so much fun just to look and to smell: to gaze at the brightly colored goods filling the store's shelves and hanging from the ceiling; to breathe in the rich smell of spices and the homey scent of pine soap and tobacco.

"Come with me to the store," Felicity encouraged. Elizabeth happily agreed.

Before long, the girls were on their way to Merriman's Store on Duke of Gloucester Street, with a newspaper tucked under Felicity's arm. The street ran exactly one mile, from the Capitol on the eastern end, past the Palace Green that stretched to the wrought-iron gates of the Governor's Palace, all the way to the College of William and Mary at its western end.

As soon as Felicity and Elizabeth turned the corner, they spotted their friend Fiona McLeod in front of the store. She was staring down the street at Miss Manderly's house, shading her eyes against the sun.

"She must be waiting for us to come from our lesson," said Elizabeth.

"Fiona!" Felicity called, waving. Fiona turned toward them and lifted her hand in a halfhearted wave. She didn't come to greet them, just silently watched them approach. She didn't even seem to care when two Patriot soldiers on horseback trotted past and splashed mud on her skirt.

"Something's amiss with her," Felicity said with concern.

Elizabeth agreed. "Let's go see what's wrong."

They picked up their pace, hurrying past gentlemen and ladies in brightly colored clothes and servants in homespun with turbans on their heads, all going in and out of shops.

When they reached her, Fiona said, "I thought you would never come." Her cheeks were flushed and her eyes troubled. "Your father said you would be here soon, Felicity, but it seems I've been waiting *forever.*"

Felicity didn't think this was the time to explain about the book in Widow Reed's window. "We had to get a newspaper for Father," she said. "What's wrong, Fiona?"

Fiona shook her head miserably. "Look at this." She held up a large sheet of printed paper. Felicity recognized it as one of the broadsides that often appeared in Williamsburg. Sometimes broadsides were used to advertise goods or services, sometimes to quickly get out news of an important event, and sometimes even to publicize someone's personal opinions.

One glance at the broadside told Felicity the reason for Fiona's distress. Her father's name, Fergus McLeod, was printed in bold letters across the top, and underneath, in slightly smaller letters, was a question: *Patriot or Pretender?*

"It accuses Da of being disloyal to the Patriots!" Fiona's hands doubled into fists, crushing the broadside. "It's not true, Felicity. You know it's not! Our fathers were among the first in Williamsburg to stop selling tea in their stores. Da's as strong a Patriot as anyone in Williamsburg!"

Felicity glanced uncertainly at Elizabeth. Elizabeth's head had dropped, and she was staring at her feet.

"Oh, Elizabeth, I'm sorry," Fiona said, touching Elizabeth's arm. "I forgot myself. I meant no disrespect to your father. I'm just so worried about Da. More has happened, you see, than just the broadside."

"I know you meant no offense," Elizabeth said softly. "Please tell us what else is the matter."

Fiona, her voice wavering, explained. "Early yesterday morning these broadsides appeared, as if by magic, all over Williamsburg. They were tacked up on taverns and shops, even on trees—*and* in front of Da's store. As soon as Da discovered them, he sent his apprentices around to take them all down, so not many people saw them. But while we were at supper last night, a messenger came to our house." Fiona bit her lip and glanced away. Her eyes followed the slow progress of a slave boy driving an oxcart past them in the street.

For a moment Felicity thought that Fiona had forgotten about her story. "Then what happened, Fiona?" she prodded gently.

Fiona's eyes snapped back to Felicity and Elizabeth. "The messenger," she said harshly, "brought a summons for Da. He's to appear before the Committee of Safety, to answer charges that he is disloyal to the Patriots."

Felicity felt a thump in her stomach. The Committee of Safety had governed Williamsburg since Lord Dunmore, the royal governor, had fled the city last year, and it held immense power. The committee was like a court, and it could pass sentences upon people whom it believed to be disloyal or dangerous to the Patriot cause. It was the Committee of Safety that had jailed Elizabeth's father because he was a Loyalist. Only through Grandfather's influence with Edward Pendleton, the head of the committee, had Mr. Cole been released.

Elizabeth's eyes held understanding. "Oh, Fiona," she said, "I know how you feel." Felicity could only imagine what it must have been like for Elizabeth when a messenger from the Committee of Safety came calling for *her* father.

Felicity stepped toward Fiona, wanting to show sympathy but not knowing how. "When does your father have to go before the committee?"

"In four days' time—on Monday," Fiona said. "But he's afraid the committee will be prejudiced against him because he's Scottish. He's inside the store now, asking your father for help, Felicity."

"Prejudiced against him because he's Scottish?" asked Felicity. "Surely not! Your father's store is one of the busiest in Williamsburg. Everyone knows your family. Why, your parents have been here since before you were born, Fiona."

"Da says in times like these, people forget such things." Fiona's chin was quivering. "And because so many Scots *are* Loyalists, some people lump us together and think we're all the same. Terrible things are happening to Scots in some of the colonies." She told Felicity and Elizabeth about a battle just four months before at Moore's Creek Bridge in North Carolina, where many Scottish Loyalists had been killed and the survivors—hundreds of them—hunted down and jailed. "Da's own uncle and his nephews are in jail . . . and their families left to starve."

Fiona's voice rose, cracking over tears. "Oh, Felicity and Elizabeth, I'm so frightened about what might happen to Da!"

Felicity took Fiona's hand in hers. "Don't worry. I'm certain Father will help him. Let's go inside and see."

The girls hurried up the store's wooden steps. Inside, Father and Mr. McLeod were at the front counter, talking. Above the counter, shelves rose all the way to the ceiling, displaying goods for sale—from teapots to candlesticks, from bolts of cloth to jars of sweets. Father and Mr. McLeod glanced at the girls as they came in. Father had his arms crossed, listening intently to Mr. McLeod.

Felicity saw Marcus, the slave who helped

Father at the store, restocking shelves nearby. Toward the back of the store, Ben, Father's apprentice, was waiting on a portly gentleman wearing a large wig. Near Ben, a man and woman were looking at a display of pewter dishes. Father gave Felicity a nod and a smile when she placed the newspaper in front of him on the counter. Felicity knew it would have been rude for Father to interrupt Mr. McLeod to offer her his usual warm greeting. She noticed that Father was holding a copy of the broadside.

The girls drifted over to a display of caps and bonnets within earshot of the men's conversation. Felicity picked up a lacy white cap and pretended to be interested in looking at it, but she kept her ears cocked to hear every word Mr. McLeod and Father were saying. Mr. McLeod was asking Father to appear before the committee with him, to testify on his behalf. "'Tis a huge favor I'm asking of ye," he said in his heavy Scottish accent.

"And one I'm glad to do for you," Father

replied without a moment's hesitation. "You're an honest, upstanding businessman, Fergus, and a good friend. I'm happy to do anything I can to help you."

Mr. McLeod, with his hawk nose and tall, solid build, had the fierce look of a Highland Scot. As he leaned in across the counter toward Father, the ferocity in his voice chilled Felicity. "You realize what I'm asking, don't you, man? The danger involved?"

"What danger?" Father asked.

"That you, for appearing with me—a Scotsman—will become a target as well."

2
THREATS

Felicity's throat went tight. *Could* Father get into trouble for standing up for Mr. McLeod? Might the committee think *he* was disloyal, too?

She shivered. Worse things than jailing had happened to Loyalists. She thought of Elizabeth's father, forced to leave his family and home. In some places, Loyalists had been tarred and feathered, a horrible practice in which they were dipped headfirst in a barrel of hot, sticky tar and then covered with chicken feathers and paraded through town. Nothing like that had happened in Williamsburg . . . yet.

And, Felicity told herself, nothing like that would happen to Father, even if he testified for Mr. McLeod. No one in Williamsburg could question Father's loyalty to the Patriots.

Father's reply to Mr. McLeod echoed her own thoughts. "I'm certain there's no danger either to you or to me, my friend," he said. "The committee is made up of distinguished citizens of Williamsburg, some of whom are our neighbors and friends. They should all know you're loyal to the Patriots. And the fact that you're Scottish should make no difference."

Mr. McLeod smiled thinly. "You'd be surprised to whom it makes a very *great* difference."

"Mr. Merriman!" The voice came from the back of the store. Felicity turned. The man Ben had been waiting on came striding up the aisle, past the girls. He was wearing a dark blue coat and yellow breeches and carrying a fancy walking cane with a silver boar's head on top. He strutted up to the front counter, his cane wagging like a bulldog's tail.

"Mr. Merriman," he repeated in a curt tone, "your apprentice would do well to keep his mind on his work. I'm afraid he's just lost you a sale."

"My apologies, Mr. Capps," Father replied. "I should be happy to assist you, if you please."

"Never mind," answered Mr. Capps. With a loud "harrumph," he tipped his three-cornered hat to Father and Mr. McLeod and sailed out the door.

Then Ben came walking sheepishly up the aisle. "What was that about, Ben?" Father asked him.

"I'm sorry, Mr. Merriman," Ben replied. "Mr. Capps was going on so long about the kind of fine stockings he wanted, I'm afraid my mind wandered to the customers near us who were talking about the war." Ben nodded toward the man and woman at the pewter display, still intent on their conversation. "Mr. Capps got irritated when I asked him to repeat what he'd said."

"With good reason," Father scolded. "How many times have I told you to keep your mind on your work, Ben? Sometimes your mind is as scattered as straw in the wind. And with times as hard as they are, we can't afford to lose any customers, or to make them angry—least of all someone like Mr. Capps, a member of the Committee of Safety."

"I know, Mr. Merriman," Ben said. "I promise you it won't happen again."

Mr. McLeod put a hand on Ben's shoulder. "Don't feel too bad, lad. It doesna take much to irritate Richard Capps. He got angry at me last week when I went to his store to ask him to pay back money he owes me. And he wouldna give me a single shilling." Then, beckoning to Fiona, he said, "Come, daughter. We've taken enough of Mr. Merriman's time."

Fiona said good-bye to Felicity and Elizabeth. "Come visit when you can," she told them.

Mr. McLeod took Fiona's arm to go. At the door he paused, his eyes brimming with gratitude. "Edward, I don't know how to thank you."

"Your friendship is thanks enough," Father said. "On Monday, we shall go to the hearing—together."

Father's promise stayed on Felicity's mind all afternoon. She felt torn. Part of her was happy that Father was willing to help Mr. McLeod, yet another part of her worried that something bad might happen to Father as a result. She wished she could talk to Mother about it, but she knew that it was Father's place, not hers, to tell Mother what had happened.

At supper that evening, Felicity kept hoping Father would bring up the subject of the broadside and what he had promised to do to help Mr. McLeod. But he didn't say anything about it until later, when the family was gathered in the parlor after supper.

The night had turned chilly, as even the balmiest spring days in Williamsburg some- times did. A fire burned in the fireplace, and Baby Polly slept in a cradle near its warmth. Four-year-old William was sprawled on the floor, playing with a set of toy soldiers that Grandfather had given him. Felicity and Nan were at the gaming table, playing checkers with polished peach stones for markers. In her favorite chair by the fire, Mother worked on a piece of embroidery, the brightly colored wools hanging from a loop on the arm of her chair.

Father was sitting at his desk in the corner, going through some papers. Felicity wondered if the broadside about Mr. McLeod was among them. Every time she heard the creak of Father's chair or the crinkle of shuffled papers, Felicity looked up from the checkerboard, hop- ing that he was ready to mention the broadside to Mother. At last he did.

Father pushed back his chair with a scrap- ing sound, got up, and handed a sheet of paper to Mother. *The broadside.* "My dear," he said to Mother, "I think you should have a look at this."

Felicity looked anxiously toward Mother, waiting for her response.

"Lissie," Nan said, "it's *your* turn."

Felicity had lost interest in the game. She glanced down at the board and purposely slid her peach stone to a square where Nan could jump her three times and win.

Nan put a hand to her mouth and giggled. "Lissie, look what you've done." Triumphantly she jumped Felicity's stones and took them off the board. "I win!"

"Yes, you do," said Felicity, pretending to be dismayed. "Excellent game, Nan. But the winner cleans up the board."

Beaming, Nan began scooping up the peach stones and dropping them into their little cloth bag. Felicity turned her attention to Mother. Father had lit his long-stemmed pipe, and now he was leaning against the mantel, smoking, waiting for Mother to finish reading. Finally

Mother laid the broadside down on the table beside her, which happened to be next to Felicity. "Mercy," Mother said, shaking her head sadly. "All of it is untrue, of course."

Father took a long draw on his pipe before he answered, and curiosity stabbed at Felicity. *What does the broadside say about Mr. McLeod?* she wondered. She didn't dare ask to read it. She knew that children were not supposed to meddle in adult concerns. But this involved her friend Fiona—and Father. *If only I could read just a little.*

She craned her neck to try to see the broadside better, but the printing was too blurred for her to read from a distance. All she could make out was the large print at the top—which she already knew—and the signature of the writer at the bottom: *Mr. Puller.* She didn't know anyone by that name, yet there was something about it that niggled at her.

Father blew out the smoke from his pipe, and it drifted up in a wreath over his head. "Of course the accusations are all untrue.

Nevertheless, the broadside has disturbed the Committee of Safety, and they've issued Fergus a summons. He's worried that the committee will go hard on him because he's Scottish. He asked me to appear with him at his hearing on Monday, and I've agreed."

There was a long silence, broken only by the shooting noises William was making with his toy soldiers and the crackling of the fire. Polly stirred in her sleep and smacked her tiny flowerbud lips. Even Nan was watching Mother. Mother had wrinkled her brow, as she always did when she was thinking hard about something. Then she nodded. "I think you did the right thing, Edward. Of course you should stand up for Fergus. Yet I worry—" She cut herself off without finishing.

"Go on," Father encouraged.

Mother chose her words carefully. "People may hear that you're going before the committee and misunderstand. They may believe that *your* patriotism is in question . . . and . . . it might affect business at the store. With times so hard . . ." She stopped again and glanced at Nan and Felicity.

Felicity instinctively looked away. She knew that Father's business had fallen off since the war began. Times were hard for all the Williamsburg merchants. Before the colonies had gone to war against the king, merchants had always stocked their stores with goods imported from England, but now those goods were no longer available. Yet Father's store was still one of the busiest in Williamsburg. Felicity had never given a second thought to whether the store was making enough money.

"I understand your concern," Father said. "If I help Fergus, we may indeed lose some customers. But I believe the store can get by well enough without them. In truth, I'd rather be without *them* than without good friends like McLeod."

"I heartily agree," Mother said.

Relief washed over Felicity. Why had she been so fearful that something bad would happen to Father if he helped Mr. McLeod?

Losing a few customers at the store was not so terrible. Father didn't seem concerned at all about it, and Mother only a trifle. And if they weren't worried, Felicity wasn't going to worry either.

The next afternoon, Felicity and Elizabeth went to visit Fiona after their lessons. Fiona took them outside to the formal garden, where the girls sat down on a stone bench.

In the bright sunshine of the garden, Felicity suddenly noticed how pale Fiona looked and the dark circles under her eyes, as if she hadn't slept well the night before. She asked Fiona if something else had happened to upset her.

"To tell you the truth, Felicity," Fiona said, "I'm frightened, much more than yesterday. This morning our servants came home from the market and told Ma they'd heard people talking about Da, calling him a king lover . . . and . . . and a bootlicking Scottish dog." Fiona grimaced, as if the words were painful to say.

Felicity's stomach knotted. Father had been so sure Mr. McLeod's fears were unfounded. Yet now it seemed that people *were* thinking the worst of McLeod because he was Scottish. She tried to ignore the whisper at the back of her mind that perhaps Father was also wrong about the risk to *himself.*

"Then, this afternoon," Fiona went on, "Da got a threatening letter from the person who wrote the broadside."

"From *Mr. Puller?*" Felicity couldn't believe that the man had been so bold as to write Mr. McLeod a letter.

"Is he someone your father knows?" Elizabeth asked.

"No one in Williamsburg seems to know who he is," said Fiona. "Or at least they won't tell Da if they do."

A cold finger of fear was inching up Felicity's spine. If Fiona's Da had been threatened, then maybe Father was in danger, too. "What did the letter say?"

"My parents wouldn't tell me," Fiona said, "though it frightened Ma enough that she begged Da to leave town right away. But he wouldn't do it." Fiona's voice sounded small and scared. "He said he refused to sneak away as if the accusations were true."

Felicity didn't know what to say. If she were in Fiona's place, what would she want Father to do? To go away to where he would be safe . . . or to stay at home and face some terrible risk? It was an impossible choice.

Then a thought shot through her head: *Be glad it's Fiona's father who has to make the choice, not yours.*

3

AN ANGRY MOB

Felicity was instantly ashamed. How could she be so selfish? She felt even worse when Elizabeth leaned over and hugged Fiona. "I know what it's like to miss one's father," Elizabeth said. "You must trust that your father is doing what he thinks is best, Fiona, for all of you."

Elizabeth's words seemed to cheer Fiona. She smiled. "You're right, Elizabeth. I will try to do that."

Felicity's hands lay stupidly in her lap. She felt as if she had failed Fiona. Why couldn't she have thought to say something so simple and so generous to Fiona, instead of being wrapped up in her own worries? She resolved to be a better friend in the future.

By the time Felicity and Elizabeth started home, the sun was low in the western sky. It was only a short walk from Fiona's house to Elizabeth's across from the Palace Green. The girls talked about how happy they were that Fiona had seemed to be in good spirits when they left her.

After Felicity dropped Elizabeth off, she took a shortcut through Elizabeth's garden and then through a pasture to her own street, Duke of Gloucester. Along the way, she thought hard about Elizabeth's words to Fiona, and by the time she got home, she had decided to take the advice for herself. She just had to trust Father, that he was doing what he thought was best.

When Felicity went to bed that evening, she left her window open to the cool spring breeze. In the middle of the night, she awoke with a jerk. She bolted upright in bed, listening hard. There was shouting somewhere outside!

Felicity jumped out of bed and dashed to the window. All the outbuildings behind the house—the kitchen and the smokehouse, the laundry and the stable—sat dark and silent in the night. Not even a breeze stirred through the apple trees; nothing moved on the grass below. Whatever was happening was in front, out on the street.

Not taking time to light a candle, Felicity threw on her dressing gown and hurried out into the hall. Mother and Father, in their night-clothes, were on the stairway landing below, Mother's candle casting an eerie fluttering shadow on the papered wall. Felicity joined her parents, slipping her hand into Mother's as they went down the stairs and into the parlor.

Quickly Father threw up the window sash and pushed out the shutters. The scene outside took Felicity's breath away. A huge mob of angry people moved down the street, carrying torches and lanterns. Shouts and curses filled the air.

"Oh, Edward!" Mother exclaimed, her hand at her throat.

"I pray it's not what I think it is," Father said grimly.

"What, Father?" Felicity asked, alarmed. "What are those people doing?"

Before Father could answer, the crowd outside parted for an instant, and Felicity strained to see. At the center of the mob, someone was pushing a man in a handcart. The man was big and clothed only in his long nightshirt. His bare legs, tied together, dangled over the side of the cart. With a jolt, Felicity recognized him. "It's Mr. McLeod!"

"I'm going out there to help him." Father's jaw was thrust out in the determined way that meant nothing could change his mind.

"What will you do, Edward?" Mother asked.

"Talk some sense into them, I hope."

"Be careful," Mother murmured.

Father kissed Mother's forehead. "I will, my love." Then he swept past Mother and Felicity, out of the room and up the stairs.

"Mother," Felicity asked, "those people outside . . . what will they do to Mr. McLeod?"

Mother hugged Felicity close to her.

"Perhaps this will be the worst of it. Let us hope your father can stop them."

Then they heard the sound of Father's rapid footsteps coming down the stairs. He called from the hallway, "I'm off," but was out the door before Mother or Felicity could reply.

From the window, the two of them, arm in arm, watched him go out through the front gate and melt into the night. The noise and shouting of the mob was now farther down the street.

You could become a target as well. Mr. McLeod's words to Father echoed in Felicity's mind. The twinge of fear that she'd felt before was as sharp now as a razor's edge. "Father will be safe, won't he, Mother?" Felicity asked. "And he *will* be able to help Mr. McLeod?"

Mother squeezed Felicity's shoulder. "Your father is well respected here, Lissie. If anyone can help Mr. McLeod, he can."

Then Mother insisted that they go back to bed and try to sleep. "We're not doing your father or Mr. McLeod a bit of good by standing here worrying." Felicity knew it was useless to protest, so she went upstairs with Mother and dutifully slid under the covers.

The linen sheets were cold as ice, and Felicity felt cold inside. When she closed her eyes, all she saw behind her lids were the leering, angry faces of the mob. She kept thinking of Father out there, trying to save Mr. McLeod.

Felicity couldn't stand the waiting any longer. She had to go out and see what was happening to Mr. McLeod—and to Father. Hurriedly she dressed and crept down the back stairs, out into the yard.

The moon was bright and round in the sky, casting a silvery light on the white oyster-shell path and the kitchen garden beyond. Up the street, she could hear angry voices and shouting. Then, closer by, a gate creaked. Felicity froze. She glimpsed a dark form moving along on the other side of the hedge. Someone was coming toward her! She stood poker-stiff, listening.

"Lissie," a familiar voice hissed in the dark. It was Ben!

With a leap Ben was over the hedge. The white of his shirt stood out starkly against the black night. "What are you doing out here, Felicity, at this hour?"

"Perhaps I should ask you the same question," Felicity said, a little annoyed at Ben for having startled her.

"I was on my way to see what all the shouting was about."

"I can tell you what it's about," Felicity said fiercely. "'Tis a mob bent on hurting Mr. McLeod. Father went to try to stop them, and I'm going to see what's happened to Father."

Ben's voice was sober. "You should go back inside, Lissie. This is dangerous. *I'll* go look for your father."

"No," Felicity insisted, "I'm going, too. I have to know that Father's all right."

Ben heaved a sigh. "Come on then, but stay close to me. 'Tis no place for a bit of a girl to be alone."

Ordinarily Felicity would have protested being called "a bit of a girl." Truthfully, though, she was glad to have Ben with her now.

Together Ben and Felicity hurried down Duke of Gloucester Street, past dark shops and houses and past Merriman's Store, its familiar front shadowy and strange. In some of the houses, candles winked from windows and faces could be seen peering out.

As Felicity and Ben went on, following the sound of the mob, they saw more and more people out on the street, headed in the same direction they were. Far down, at the end of Duke of Gloucester, Felicity could see the hulking shape of the Capitol building, its cupola white against the night sky. As they neared the King's Arms Tavern, the small stream of people became a flood that filled the street and merged with the mob in front of the two-storied tavern. Ben saw his friend Walter in the crowd, and he and Felicity pushed toward him.

Ben grabbed Walter's arm to get his attention. "What's happening?" he asked Walter, almost having to shout to be heard.

"I don't know," Walter said. "I'm trying to find out myself."

Quickly Ben told Walter what they knew about the mob and said that he and Felicity were trying to find Felicity's father. The three of them moved along the edge of the throng, trying to get closer to the tavern steps, where most of the crowd was massed.

From the midst of the mob rang harsh voices, shouts, and curses that made Felicity's skin prickle. What were these people doing to Mr. McLeod? Or had the mob turned on *Father?* Suddenly panic choked her and she bolted forward, trying to thrust her way into the crush of people to find Father.

Ben seized her arm and pulled her back. "Are you daft, girl? What do you think you're doing?"

Felicity struggled to break from Ben's grasp. "Let me go! I have to find Father!"

"Lissie!" Ben grabbed her shoulders and held tightly. "You can't find him in this crowd.

And you need to stay with us. It's dangerous! D'you understand?" All around them was a chaos of shrill voices, hoarse laughter, shouting, and people milling around them and pushing past them.

"He's right," Walter said grimly. "Mobs like this can turn ugly in a heartbeat."

Felicity's eyes were blurring with tears. "But what if they've done something to Father? Please, Ben, I need to know what's happening."

For a moment Ben considered. Not far away, a multitude of voices erupted in angry howls. "Please, Ben," Felicity begged.

Ben gave a tight nod. "We'll try to get closer." He and Walter, shielding Felicity between them, shouldered through the mob toward the front of the crowd.

Desperately, Felicity's eyes roved the crowd, searching for Father. But most of the faces were only shadows, their features impossible to distinguish in the dark. Here and there a lantern speckled a face or clothes with dim yellow light.

Then Felicity caught sight of something that sent a shudder through her body. Under the eave of the tavern's front stoop, lighted by a single lantern, sat a steaming barrel of tar. Its sharp, hot odor filled her nostrils. Beside the barrel was a bag stuffed full of downy goose feathers, some of the feathers swirling up and out of the bag in the evening's gusty breeze.

In a sickening instant she knew: the mob planned to tar and feather Mr. McLeod. For whatever reason, she thought with relief, it hadn't happened yet.

Felicity exchanged a glance with Ben and Walter that told her they had reached the same conclusion she had. Near the stoop Felicity saw the handcart that had given Mr. McLeod his roughshod ride. It was empty. There was no sign of Mr. McLeod anywhere, or of Father.

Felicity's stomach clenched. *Where are they?*

Just as she was about to put her question to Ben and Walter, two shabbily dressed men and a coarse-looking woman jostled past them, speaking gruffly to one another. "The king-loving dog got away free and clear," one of the ruffians muttered. "If it had been up to me, I'd 'ave seen him hanged."

"Or at least run out of town on a fence rail," the woman threw in.

"There's always another night to get even with a traitorous Scot," said the second man.

"Aye," growled the first man, "and the turncoat who took his side."

Felicity's head snapped around to look at them. They were talking about Mr. McLeod and Father! For an instant she felt dizzy with relief and fear. Then she realized that Ben was talking to her. "Did you hear?" he was saying. "Your father must have saved Mr. McLeod."

Her mind whirling, all Felicity could do was nod.

"Likely he's taking Mr. McLeod home," Ben said. "And the sooner I get you home, Lissie, the better."

Felicity couldn't shift her thoughts away

from the threatening words of the ruffians.
It sounded as if they wouldn't be satisfied
until harm had been done to Mr. McLeod—
and to Father.

"Will you be all right getting Felicity
home?" Walter asked Ben. "You know I go
in the opposite direction."

Ben assured Walter they'd be fine, and
then he and Felicity started home. Once they
were past Merriman's Store, the noise of the
mob faded, and the streets were dark and
quiet. Soon they came in sight of Felicity's
house, where a light was burning in the parlor
window. "Father must be home!" Felicity cried.

They hurried up the shell path to the steps
and through the front door. Felicity rushed into
the parlor, expecting to see Father. Instead, she
found Mother dozing in the wing chair by the
hearth, a piece of embroidery on her lap.

Mother awoke suddenly. "Edward?" Then
her eyes widened. "Lissie! And Ben! What on
earth—?" Her words were cut off by the thud
of the front door and the scuff of feet in the

hall. Then Father was standing in the parlor doorway. His face and clothes were streaked with dirt.

A thrill skipped through Felicity. Father was safe!

Mother bowed her head for a moment. When she looked up, her eyes brimmed with tears. "Oh, Edward," she said, "do come in." It wasn't like Mother to show an excess of emotion, but Felicity could hear the heartfelt relief in her words.

Felicity didn't try to hold back her own feelings. "Father, I'm so glad you're home!" In a few steps, she was in his arms. He smelled of sweat and smoke and tar, but wonderfully like Father. He hugged her and kissed the top of her head.

Then he was in the room, Mother embracing him and Ben asking him about Mr. McLeod. Before Father could answer, Mother made everyone sit down so that Father could rest. Father explained how he had gotten to the tavern in time to stop the mob from harming

Mr. McLeod and convinced them to let him take Mr. McLeod home.

With a grim expression, Ben told Father about the ruffians' threats against Mr. McLeod. Anxiously Felicity watched Father for his reaction.

Something flickered in Father's eyes. Worry? Anger? Fear? Before Felicity could read it, the look was gone. "I should warn him," Father said. Swiping his hand through his hair, he stood up.

But there was more Felicity wanted him to know. Abruptly she stood and went to his side. "Father, they talked about coming to get you, too." Felicity looked into Father's eyes and tried not to let her voice break. "Because you stood up for Mr. McLeod."

The candle on the table beside the settee fluttered in a draft and made Father's shadow jump across the wall. "Edward, you don't think—" Mother started.

"No, I don't," Father said firmly. "Everyone in town knows the work I do for the Patriots."

He touched Mother's shoulder in a gesture of comfort.

Then he turned away from Mother, strode to the hearth, and laid a hand on the mantel. "I fear for Fergus McLeod, though. All over the colonies, neighbor is turning against neighbor, family against family. Innocent people are being hurt. Sadly, 'tis part and parcel of war."

Ben sat up ramrod-straight. "That's no reason for us to accept it, sir!"

"Nor do I intend to," Father said. "The whole business started with the broadside attacking McLeod, published by this rascal calling himself Puller—a man whom no one in Williamsburg seems to know."

Mr. Puller. Once again that name tugged at Felicity. But why?

"'Tis likely a false name," Father was going on. "I shall do what I can to find out who's hiding behind it. In the meantime, I intend to fight Mr. Puller with the sword of his own choosing."

"How can you fight him, Father," Felicity

asked, "if you don't even know who he is?"

"With words, my dear daughter, in print—
words that I hope will restore McLeod's reputation among the citizens of Williamsburg.
Tomorrow I shall go to Widow Reed's and
place an advertisement defending him in next
week's issue of the *Gazette.*"

Felicity tried to ignore the tickle of
worry inside her. Words in print had started
McLeod's troubles. She sorely hoped the same
wouldn't start trouble for Father.

4

AN OLD FRIEND

"Lissie." Felicity climbed out of a deep sleep and opened her eyes. Nan was gently shaking her. "Mother sent me to wake you," Nan said. "You've missed breakfast, but Rose is keeping it warm for you in the kitchen."

Felicity was suddenly wide-awake. Mother had let her sleep through breakfast? That was unheard-of. Then she remembered last night. *The mob. Father threatened.*

Nan was going on. "You're to go with Mother to the market this morning. I wanted to go, too, but Mother said I must stay and mind William and Polly so that Rose can see to the spinning. And Mother said I'm not to pester you with any questions." Nan bit her lip and screwed up her face, as if trying to squeeze back the questions she was dying to ask.

Felicity was amused in spite of herself. "Thank you, Nan. Tell Mother I'll be down straightaway."

When Nan had left, Felicity, bleary-eyed, climbed out of bed and started to dress. Last night seemed like a terrible nightmare. Felicity's worry about whether the men would come back for Father gnawed at her like a dog chewing a bone, reminding her just how real last night was.

The gnawing stayed with Felicity as she and Mother walked to the market square behind the courthouse. Once there, Felicity scanned the faces of the people she saw and wondered whether they had been part of last night's mob. Scarier still, she wondered whether the ringleaders themselves were here someplace among the market's crowded stalls.

When Felicity noticed a man staring at Mother, Fiona's words came sharply to her mind: *the market . . . people talking about Da . . .* Felicity looked more closely at the man. What did he want with Mother? Had *he* been in the mob? Had he seen Father rescue Mr. McLeod? She glanced anxiously at Mother. Mother hadn't seen the man; she was bent over a cart piled with baskets of spring vegetables and herbs.

Then the man walked over to them. "Excuse me, madame," he said. Mother looked up from the vegetables, and the man's face lit up. "Martha Merriman! It *is* you! What a pleasure this is!" He swept the tricornered hat off his nearly bald head and bowed so low that his walking cane almost touched the ground. Then he rose and kissed Mother's hand. "I see that the years have only increased your loveliness."

Mother smiled graciously. "John Sutherland! 'Tis a great pleasure to see you as well. I'd heard you had moved back to Williamsburg."

Felicity felt the tension drain out of her. The man was somebody Mother knew!

"Indeed," he said. "I've opened a grocery store on Nicholson Street. When my dear wife passed away, I found that I could no longer bear life in Baltimore without her. You knew that my wife had died, did you not?"

Mother said she had heard that sad news and offered her sympathy. Then she introduced Felicity. Mr. Sutherland looked down at Felicity and smiled. "Ah, young miss, I note the beauty of the mother in the daughter."

Felicity felt herself go red in the face. She didn't quite know how to respond to his comment, which was less a greeting than another compliment to Mother. "How do you do," she said shyly.

Mother and Mr. Sutherland continued chatting a while longer, Mother telling him about her family and Mr. Sutherland going on about Mother's youthful appearance. At last the conversation seemed to be ending. Mother invited Mr. Sutherland to come for coffee one day soon, and Mr. Sutherland promised he would do so as soon as his thriving business allowed. When he was gone, Felicity asked, "Who was that man, Mother?"

"Mr. Sutherland is a very old friend," she

said. "Your father and I have known him since we were young. But come now. Rose will be wondering what has become of us."

Felicity nodded and followed Mother through the maze of carts and people. Mother's response had only made Felicity more curious about Mr. Sutherland. If he knew Father, too, why had Mr. Sutherland not asked about him? Though Mr. Sutherland had been pleasant enough, Felicity didn't think she cared much for him. She hoped his business would keep him too occupied to come for coffee anytime soon.

After they left the market, Felicity asked if they could visit Fiona and her mother, since the McLeods' house was so near, just across the Palace Green. "I think that is a fine idea," Mother said. A flock of sheep grazing on the lush grass of the Palace Green scattered before Mother and Felicity as they walked across.

At the McLeods' house, Mother lifted the brass knocker and rapped on the front door. There was no answer, so Mother knocked again.

Still no one came to the door. That seemed odd to Felicity. The McLeods had several servants, as well as three slaves who cooked and gardened and kept the stables for them. There was always someone available to answer the door.

"No one is home, it seems," Mother said.

"Why doesn't one of the servants answer?" Felicity wondered aloud.

"I don't know." Mother sounded as perplexed as Felicity was. "But there's nothing for us to do except go home."

A nervous feeling fluttered in Felicity's stomach. The house was so strangely quiet, and the downstairs curtains were all drawn. There was not even a sound from the kitchen or stables behind the house. "Do you think there's anything to be concerned about?" she asked Mother.

Mother's face clouded, and she hesitated a moment. "Probably not," she finally said. "It was a long night for the McLeods. It could be that everyone is still asleep."

Felicity knew that was unlikely; judging by the sun overhead, it was nearly noon. As they turned to leave, Felicity glanced up at Fiona's bedchamber window on the second floor. She was startled to see Fiona's troubled face staring down at her. An instant later, the face was gone.

"Mother, they *are* home!" Felicity said. "I saw Fiona at the window, and I know she saw me. Why wouldn't she come to the door?"

"Fiona and her parents have been through a terrible shock," Mother said. "Perhaps they're not ready to receive company. We'll come back in a few days."

For the rest of the day, Felicity couldn't get the image of Fiona's face out of her mind. She told Ben about it that evening before supper, when the two of them were in the stable taking care of Penny and Patriot. Penny was Felicity's mare, and Patriot was Penny's colt, born only a few months ago.

Ben measured out oats for Penny with a large wooden scoop while Felicity groomed Penny's copper-colored coat and Patriot pressed close to Penny's side. "'Twas as if Fiona *wanted* me to see her," Felicity said as she brushed Penny's glossy neck, "yet she wouldn't come to the door."

Ben stepped past Felicity to pour Penny's oats into the feed trough. "Maybe Fiona *couldn't* come," he suggested, "for whatever reason."

Felicity heaved a worried sigh. "That's what I wish I knew, Ben. The reason."

At that moment, Walter appeared in the stable doorway. "I was making a delivery nearby for our store," he said, "and thought I'd drop by to make sure you two got home safely last night. By the looks of you, you did. Is Mr. Merriman all right, and Mr. McLeod?"

Ben assured him that both men were safe. Then Ben explained to Felicity that Walter was also a storekeeper's apprentice and that his master was Mr. Capps. "You had the pleasure of meeting Mr. Capps in your father's store the other day, Lissie," Ben said with a note of sarcasm. "He chewed me up and spit me out because I wasn't paying careful attention to him, remember?"

"Oh, yes," Felicity said, nodding heartily.

Walter shook his head at Ben's story. "You never know *what* will set Capps off. The man is the devil to work for. I'm right glad, I tell you, whenever he goes on one of his trips to Portsmouth—though I don't know how he can afford to be away so much. Business at the store is so poor, we scarcely have any customers at all. Yet Capps always seems able to pull a gold coin or two out of the store's moneybox."

Walter reached out his hand for Penny to sniff. When Penny gave an approving snort, he stroked her muzzle. "If Capps wasn't such a Patriot and a member of the Committee of Safety, I'd think he was selling to some rich Loyalist in Portsmouth. They're the only ones with British gold these days."

"If that's true," said Ben, "Mr. Capps had

better hope that word doesn't get to Williamsburg about it, or his store really will have no business."

Just then Nan came to the stable to call Felicity and Ben to supper, so Walter took his leave. At supper, Father broke sad news: Mr. McLeod had sent word to Father that he and his family were leaving Williamsburg for good.

Felicity set her fork down on her plate. Her appetite had suddenly disappeared. "When, Father?" she asked.

"They're already gone," Father replied. "They left for Yorktown this afternoon with plans to board a ship bound for Boston, where they have relatives. Fergus was afraid of trouble, so they left town in secret."

That was why Fiona didn't come to the door, Felicity thought. Fiona's family must have been preparing to leave at any moment and didn't want anyone to know. Briefly Felicity's eyes met Mother's, and understanding shot between them.

Father went on. "Fergus thought I ought to know, since the Committee of Safety hearing is on Monday, two days from now, and he saw no need for me to risk testifying for him. I suppose he has lost faith in the good people of Williamsburg."

"I can't say that I blame him," Mother said.

Father sighed. "I wish he hadn't been so hasty in leaving. I went to Widow Reed's this morning and arranged to place a defense of him in next Thursday's *Gazette.* The ill feeling against him, I think, would have died down after he had a chance to clear his name at the hearing, and after people read my defense of him. But now that he's left town, 'twill seem he was guilty, and the committee is likely to rule against him."

"But there's nothing they can do to him now that he's gone!" Felicity burst out.

"Not to him personally," Father replied, "but the Committee *can* take his property, and that's what they'll probably do. Most likely the McLeods' house and store will be sold at public auction."

A lump of misery lodged itself in Felicity's throat. How unjust it seemed! Fiona was gone forever, and her family's property would soon belong to someone else.

And Felicity hadn't even had a chance to say good-bye.

5

PUBLIC AUCTION

Father's ad in the *Gazette* defending Mr. McLeod came out on Thursday. But it was too late. On Monday, the Committee of Safety had ruled that Mr. McLeod was guilty of disloyalty, and all of his property was to be sold to benefit the Patriot cause. Everything had happened just the way Father had predicted.

On Friday, Felicity went with Father to the auction in front of the McLeods' house. A huge crowd had gathered to watch, spilling out across the street into the Palace Green. It seemed to Felicity that nearly everyone in Williamsburg must be there. Just then, a man in a large powdered wig jostled Felicity with his cane as he pushed toward the front of the crowd. "Pardon me, miss," he said.

Felicity looked at him sharply. Where had she heard that voice before? Then it occurred to her. It was Mr. Sutherland, from the market—Mother's old friend. Felicity hadn't recognized him because today he was wearing such a thick, heavy wig.

Then Mr. Sutherland glanced at Father, seeming to recognize him for the first time. "Why, Edward Merriman, how do you do, old fellow?"

Felicity felt annoyance stirring. Mr. Sutherland's tone held a note of arrogance, as if he thought he was Father's superior.

Father didn't seem bothered by it. "John," he said heartily, clasping Mr. Sutherland's hand, "I'm right glad to see you. It's been a long while since we've met."

"Aye, many years." Mr. Sutherland nodded, though his eyes were darting into the crowd rather than focusing on Father.

Who is he looking for? Felicity wondered.

"I welcome you back to Williamsburg," Father said.

"Thank you most kindly," Mr. Sutherland replied. "We shall have to talk soon. For now, I must hurry up to the auction block. I plan to place a bid on the store that is being auctioned. Good day." He tipped his tricornered hat and moved away into the crowd.

The store that is being auctioned. How cold and impersonal Mr. Sutherland made it sound. Felicity knew that he had probably not known Mr. McLeod, since he had been gone from Williamsburg so many years. Yet somehow his words had a bitter taste.

Soon the auction began. With a heavy heart, Felicity watched as the McLeods' possessions were sold off one by one. Then the house itself was sold. It was unusually large for Williamsburg, and there weren't many bidders on it. In the end, the house sold for far below its worth to Alexander Ramsey, one of the Williamsburg printers.

Mr. Ramsey was a beefy man with a red, bulbous nose that reminded Felicity of an ill-shaped turnip. After the auctioneer had awarded the McLeod house to him, someone from the crowd shouted out, "Ain't none too soon, eh, Ramsey?"

Mr. Ramsey, who was Scottish like the McLeods, replied in his thick accent, "Aye, laddie, we're busting at the seams as it is!"

The crowd laughed. Mr. Ramsey already had ten children, and his wife, Felicity knew, had recently had a baby. She had overheard Mother talking about what a difficult time Mrs. Ramsey had had with her pregnancy and the birth.

Finally, the auctioneer announced the sale of Mr. McLeod's store. For a while there was furious bidding. At last the bidding came down to two men—Walter's master, Mr. Capps, and Mr. Sutherland.

As the bids went higher and higher, Felicity noticed Mr. Capps's face getting redder and redder. She remembered what Mr. McLeod had said about how easily Capps got angry. She felt sorry for Walter having to work for such a man. At last, Mr. Capps threw up his hands and barked, "Take it, sir! No store in Williamsburg is worth that much!"

Mr. Sutherland smiled gleefully. "Time will tell, won't it, my good man?" He held out his hand for Mr. Capps to shake, but Capps only glowered at him. Then he turned and with an insistent "Pardon me, please!" pushed away into the crowd.

It was over so fast, Felicity thought. In a matter of minutes, Mr. McLeod's store had become Mr. Sutherland's. She asked Father what he thought Mr. Sutherland would do with the store now that it was his.

"I expect he has plans to expand his grocery store," Father replied. "Whatever he does, I'm sure he'll make a success of it. I've known John Sutherland since we were boys in school, there in the Wren building." Father nodded toward the main building of the College of William and Mary a few blocks away. Three stories tall, the redbrick, ivy-covered structure was visible from all over Williamsburg.

"John has always had a way of getting what

he wanted," Father went on. "Except in one very important matter."

"What was that, Father?" Felicity asked.

"Once upon a time," Father said with a twinkle in his eye, "John and I were both suitors for your mother's hand. I, of course, was the happy winner of that contest."

Now Felicity understood Mr. Sutherland's fawning over Mother. He had once wanted to marry her! Felicity slipped her hand into Father's large one. "I'm glad you were the winner, Father."

Smiling, Father gave Felicity's fingers a gentle squeeze. "So am I, Lissie. Let's go home."

Felicity was glad to go. The auction of the McLeods' house and store had been far too sad. As they started to leave, Mr. Whythe, a friend of Father's, came up to Father and caught him by the arm. "Thank God I've found you, Merriman," he said, looking grim. "Have you seen this yet?" He shoved a printed sheet of paper into Father's hand.

Another broadside.

Felicity felt a rush of anger. Would people never leave Mr. McLeod alone? Then she saw the broadside's headline written in bold—*McLeod and Merriman: Partners in Misdeeds.*

Felicity's heart lurched. The broadside was about Father!

And it was signed by Mr. Puller.

Father handed the broadside back to Mr. Whythe. "There's no truth to any of this," he said evenly. Yet his eyes were smoldering.

"I know that, man," Mr. Whythe replied. "But in these troubled times, all it takes is the suggestion of wrongdoing to make it so in some people's eyes. Look what happened to McLeod."

Father glanced down at Felicity. "You've lessons, have you not, Lissie? Better get along."

It wasn't time for Felicity's lessons, but she understood that Father wanted to talk to Mr. Whythe privately. She left them and started for home, her chest tight with anger toward this Mr. Puller.

Who is he? she seethed. *And what does he have against Father and Mr. McLeod?*

Clenching her fists, Felicity vowed to find out. Perhaps Elizabeth would help her. She was almost home, but she turned around and headed back to Elizabeth's house. On the way, she picked up one of the hateful broadsides that someone had thrown down on the street.

Felicity took her usual shortcut to Elizabeth's. A brisk wind drove clouds across the sky and sent a white shower of dogwood petals fluttering off the trees that lined the Coles' picket fence.

Felicity spotted Elizabeth wearing gloves and a wide-brimmed straw hat, weeding the flower garden. The flowers, set in large square beds, had put forth a blaze of colors. The blooms smelled sweet and sharp in the late-afternoon sun.

Felicity filled Elizabeth in on what had happened at the auction and showed her the broadside. She told Elizabeth that Father believed Puller was a false name. "Somehow

I'm going to find out who Mr. Puller really is. Will you help me?"

"Of course," said Elizabeth. "Two heads are always better than one. Let's take a closer look at the broadside. Maybe there's something in it that will give us a clue."

The girls settled on a bench in the arbor next to the flower garden. Felicity smoothed the crumpled paper on her lap and the girls bent forward to read it. "The ink is so blurred, it's hard to make out some of the words," Elizabeth commented.

Felicity nodded. "The broadside about Mr. McLeod was blurry, too."

"Maybe that's a clue in itself," Elizabeth said. "But what would it mean?"

"That both broadsides were printed on the same press?" Felicity wondered aloud. "But that doesn't tell us much if we don't know whose press it was."

Elizabeth wrinkled her brow. "Mr. Puller. There must be some significance to that name. It seems to me I've heard it before."

A gust of wind made Felicity shiver. Something stirred in the back of her mind, something that had niggled at her each time she had heard Mr. Puller's name. She screwed up her face, struggling hard to retrieve the memory. At last it came to her. "We *did* hear that name, Elizabeth! Remember when we were looking at *Gulliver's Travels* in Widow Reed's window, and we heard her calling out to her apprentices?"

"Yes!" Elizabeth said, her eyes bright with sudden understanding. "She called one of them Puller, didn't she?"

"And the other one Beater," Felicity said. "But not because those were their *names.* Mistress Reed showed me around her shop once, and she told me that the people who operate the printing press are called a beater and a puller. It's something to do with the tasks they perform."

"So whoever wrote the broadsides must know something about printing," Elizabeth concluded. "Do you think, then, that one of the Williamsburg printers is Mr. Puller?"

"It's likely either that or he's someone who works in one of the print shops," Felicity agreed.

"It can't be Widow Reed," Elizabeth said. "She's your father's friend, isn't she?"

"So are Mr. Ramsey and Mr. Hunter," Felicity pointed out, mentioning the names of the other two master printers. "It just doesn't make sense. I can't imagine any of them doing something like this—allowing such lies to be printed on their presses."

"Nor can I," said Elizabeth. "But it had to be printed somewhere. Why don't we visit all the printers' shops and ask them if they know anything about it? Maybe something they say will give us another clue."

Felicity agreed that it was a good idea, and the girls made plans to go to the print shops tomorrow. A patter of rain had begun to fall, and Elizabeth's mother called her to come in.

As Felicity hurried home, the drizzle became a downpour, and an early dusk set in. Other people were rushing along the street, eager to get out of the rain. The colorful feathers on women's hats were soggy and drooping, and the brims of men's tricornered hats poured out water like funnels. Rain soaked Felicity's straw hat and the linen cap underneath and ran in little rivers down her face. It soaked her frock right down to her shift, soaked her stockings and her shoes. To make matters worse, a chilly wind started to blow.

By the time Felicity got home, she was drenched and shivering. Mother helped Felicity strip off her cold, dripping clothes and hang them on pegs by the hearth to dry. She gave Felicity an early supper in front of the fire and sent her to bed.

Felicity slept fitfully, her rest broken by uneasy dreams. Each time she woke, the same questions were racing through her mind: *Who is Mr. Puller? Is he one of the Williamsburg*

printers? Why does someone want to hurt Father?

At last Felicity gave up trying to sleep. She lit a candle and looked for the book she was reading, Father's copy of *Pilgrim's Progress.* Then she remembered she'd been reading in the parlor a couple of nights ago; she must have left the book there. She slipped on her dressing gown and glided down the stairs.

Mother and Father were still up. The low drone of their voices came from the parlor, and a soft flickering light from the fireplace spilled out into the hallway where Felicity stood. She hesitated, not sure whether she should interrupt her parents' conversation.

Mother was talking to Father about Mrs. Ramsey, the wife of the printer who'd bought the McLeods' house. "Mrs. Ramsey has been ill ever since she delivered the baby," Mother was saying. "Childbirth fever." The rapid *click-click* of Mother's knitting needles never once slowed as she spoke.

"Yes, I know." Father's voice was a bit farther away than Mother's. Felicity guessed that he was sitting at his desk in the corner. "Ramsey told me yesterday, when he came to ask me to pay back some money I owe him. Said he hated to ask but was sorely in need of cash."

"How much do you owe him?" Mother asked.

Father mentioned a sum that Felicity couldn't quite make out.

"That much?" The clicking of Mother's needles suddenly stopped. "How will you pay him, Edward, with business slack at the store and cash money so hard to come by?"

Felicity blew out her candle and stepped closer to hear the answer, pressing against the wall to keep from being seen.

"I'll *find* a way to pay him," Father said with an edge to his voice. He sighed and then went on more quietly. "Ramsey wouldn't have asked if he didn't need the money badly. I imagine he was trying to gather the money to bid on the McLeods' house at the auction—and, of course, to pay the apothecary's fees for his wife."

There was a long pause. All Felicity heard was the snapping of the fire and the ticking of the tall clock in the hallway. Finally Mother said, "Forgive me, Edward, for worrying. I've let the broadside and the talk against you distress me when it shouldn't."

Felicity tensed. *What talk against Father?* She waited, her heart pounding, hoping Mother would say more.

"Those women at the market who said they wouldn't shop with you anymore . . ." Mother said. "To think they questioned your loyalty to the Patriot cause!"

A chair creaked. "Wife." Father's voice was gentle. Felicity imagined him leaning closer to Mother. "You needn't fear. We may lose a few customers because of the broadside. But most of my customers know me well as a Patriot and a trustworthy man; I've no doubt of that."

Mother sighed. "Nor have I."

"But there is something else that concerns me." Father's chair scraped the floor. He was standing up. Through the crack between the parlor doors, Felicity saw him walk in front of the fireplace and then turn to face Mother. Quickly Felicity pushed herself into the corner on the other side of the clock, where Father couldn't see her. She knew it was wrong to eavesdrop, but she wanted to hear what Father had to say.

The flickering light of the fire showed deep lines in Father's face. "My mail has been tampered with. After I left the auction, I went by Ramsey's to pick up a letter he said was waiting for me at his shop." Felicity knew Father meant the post office in Mr. Ramsey's print shop. "The seal on the letter had been broken and resealed. I didn't notice it until I opened the letter at home."

"You don't think Mr. Ramsey—?"

"No," Father said. "I'm sure Mr. Ramsey had nothing to do with it."

"Then who? This *Mr. Puller?*" Her tone was scornful.

"Perhaps," Father replied. "Whoever Mr. Puller is." Felicity heard the thud of Father

thrusting the poker against a log in the fireplace. "At any rate, tomorrow I must leave
town for several days to attend to some business. Ben will sleep here in the house while
I'm gone."

"You don't expect trouble?" Mother said,
anxiety tingeing her voice.

Images of the angry mob flashed into
Felicity's mind. She strained to hear Father's
response.

"I don't expect it," Father replied. "But
'tis always better to be safe."

"Must you go *now,* Edward?" Mother
asked quietly. "With all that's been happening
here?" Felicity knew that Mother would
never question Father unless she was really
worried.

"The business is pressing," Father said
sharply. His tone discouraged further questions, and Mother fell silent. The click of her
needles resumed, but much more slowly than
before. Felicity heard Father's heavy footsteps
treading across the room and then a loud

thump and a creak, as if Father had thrown himself back into his chair.

It isn't like Father to be short-tempered. And it isn't like Mother to question Father's decisions. Something was terribly wrong.

And Felicity was sure it had to do with Mr. Puller.

6
TROUBLE FOR FATHER

When Felicity woke up in the morning, she could hardly breathe. Her chest felt tight, and her head felt as if it were stuffed with cotton. Mother made a mustard plaster to place on Felicity's chest to help her breathe more easily. "You'll not budge from this bed until you're well," Mother declared.

"But Mother," Felicity protested, her voice little more than a croak, "Elizabeth and I have plans." They had to find out who Mr. Puller was!

"Whatever you and Elizabeth planned can wait," Mother said firmly. Felicity wanted to say that what she had to do *couldn't* wait, but a coughing spell cut off her words. Then Mother went on. "I shall have Rose bring up some herb tea, and I want you to drink every drop. Do you hear me?"

Felicity nodded. When Mother had that tone in her voice, it was useless to argue.

Promising that she would send word to Elizabeth that Felicity was sick, Mother left the room.

Felicity stared in frustration out the window. Why did she have to get sick now?

The next day was Sunday, and Felicity was still sick. Mother didn't go to church, but instead stayed home to take care of Felicity. By evening, Felicity was so much improved, Mother allowed her to join the family downstairs in the parlor after supper. The only thing Mother said about Father's absence was that he was away on business.

Felicity sat in Mother's wing chair, wrapped in blankets, and read *Pilgrim's Progress*. Mother was sewing, as usual, and Ben played a game of jackstraws on the floor with Nan and William until it was time for them to go to bed. When Mother left to take them upstairs, Ben confided to Felicity that he was worried about something that had happened at the store the day before. "I've misplaced your father's ledger," he confessed.

Felicity gave a little gasp. The ledger book was where Father kept track of all the store's accounts, what goods had been paid for and what money was still owed. If the ledger book was lost, it would be a disaster for the store. "Oh, Ben," Felicity said with sympathy, "Father will be furious."

"That's why I have to find it before he gets back," Ben said. "You must get well quickly and help me look for it. It's got to be in the store's office somewhere. I was making entries in it only yesterday morning at your father's desk. But when I went back to look for it later, I couldn't find it."

"That doesn't sound so bad," Felicity said. "You probably just put the ledger somewhere without thinking, and now you've forgotten where. We'll find it."

"We have to," Ben said. "It will never do for your father to know I've been absentminded again." Then he grinned. "And speaking of that, guess who came into the store yesterday?"

"Who?" Felicity asked.

"My friend, Mr. Capps," Ben said sarcastically. "You'll be happy to know, Lissie, that I was most patient with him—even though he had me search through stacks of ready-made clothing and shoes for just the right style, only to decide not to buy anything at all. I was annoyed, I admit, but I didn't let on."

"Good for you, Ben," Felicity said. "Father would be proud of you for that."

Finally, on Tuesday morning, Felicity was well enough that Mother allowed her to visit Elizabeth. Felicity had kept one of the broadsides against Father, and, before leaving for

Elizabeth's, she slipped it into the pocket that was tied around her waist under her skirt. She wanted to be able to show the broadside to the printers, just in case they hadn't seen it.

First Felicity went by the store to help Ben look for Father's account book. When she walked in, she was surprised to see Ben at the front counter writing in the ledger. "You found it!" she exclaimed.

"Aye," Ben said. "It was the strangest thing. I got to the store early this morning to have another look for the ledger before any customers came in. I sat down at your father's desk to go through it again, and there was the ledger, stuffed into one of the desk's compartments in plain view. I must have been a ninny not to have seen it before."

"You know how it is when you're desperately looking for something," Felicity said. "You sometimes miss what's right under your nose."

"That's true. Yet I could swear I looked in every drawer and compartment in that desk two or three times and didn't see it."

"Oh, well," Felicity said, "the important thing is that you've found it now."

"And none too soon. Your father said he'd be returning in three or four days' time—"

"And today's the fourth day," Felicity finished for Ben. "Good. I've missed Father terribly!"

Felicity left the store in good spirits. Father was sure to be home today, and she had high hopes that she and Elizabeth would find out something useful about Mr. Puller at one of the printers' shops.

Elizabeth suggested that they go first to Mr. Hunter's, since it was closest to her house, but Mr. Hunter's shop was so full of customers, the girls decided to come back later. Next they went to Mr. Ramsey's on Duke of Gloucester Street.

When they came in, Mr. Ramsey was hurrying from the back room, talking over his shoulder to a tall yellow-haired boy working at a table—his apprentice, Felicity guessed. "I dinna *know* when I'll be back, I tell you. Surely, lad, you can do *something* without my help."

The boy made a reply that Felicity couldn't hear. Mr. Ramsey turned around and glared at him. "For pity's sake, lad, try!" he exclaimed. Then, in a gesture of frustration, he threw up his hands and made for the door.

"Please, sir—" Felicity began, trying to get Mr. Ramsey's attention.

Mr. Ramsey held up a hand to stop her from speaking and, without a word, huffed past her, nearly barreling into a man who had just come in the shop. Felicity almost groaned out loud. The man was Mr. Capps.

"Watch your step, man!" Capps said.

"Oh, Mr. Capps! I do apologize," Mr. Ramsey said. "I was on my way out, and I must hurry, I'm afraid. Zachary will be happy to assist you."

"Oh, yes, yes, Zachary," muttered Capps. "How is he—"

"I'm sorry, Mr. Capps," Mr. Ramsey broke in. "I must leave immediately! My wife isna doing well at all." Ramsey shot an impatient glance over his shoulder. "Zachary, get out here at once!" he demanded. Then, without waiting for Zachary to appear, Ramsey snatched his tricornered hat from a peg on the wall, grabbed his walking cane, and hurried out.

The door slammed behind him, and the bell above it tinkled furiously. Felicity, standing next to Mr. Capps, saw his lips go tight with anger.

Then Zachary shuffled out from the back room, looking as if he'd just gotten out of bed. His clothes were wrinkled, his waistcoat was buttoned wrong, and his hair was doing its best to escape from the leather tie that pulled it back. "Yes, sir—" the boy began, looking at Mr. Capps.

"Oh, go ahead and help the young ladies," Capps growled.

Zachary, stifling a yawn, turned to Felicity and Elizabeth. "May I help you, please?"

Felicity hesitated. Should she ask Zachary about the broadside? An apprentice often knew nearly as much about his master's business as the master did himself. But Mr. Capps was drumming his fingers on the counter and heaving impatient sighs, and Felicity didn't want to risk irritating him further.

"No, thank you," she said to Zachary. He gave a disinterested shrug and turned back to Mr. Capps.

"Come on, Elizabeth," Felicity muttered, and the two of them left the shop.

Back out on the street, men in jaunty hats hurried past them on their way to the wig maker's and the King's Arms Tavern nearby.

"*That* was useless," Elizabeth said, looking as frustrated as Felicity felt.

"For certain," Felicity agreed. "As useless as Mr. Ramsey's apprentice seems to be." Then she added bitterly, "We haven't found out *anything,* nor even been able to ask a single question. We've wasted the whole morning."

"We've plenty of time yet to go to Widow Reed's," Elizabeth reassured her. "She'll talk to us, no matter how busy she is."

The girls walked as fast as they could to

Widow Reed's. Before they went in, Felicity, out of habit, glanced at the shop's window for a look at *Gulliver's Travels.* But the book wasn't there! In its place was a cheap-looking paperbound copy of a book entitled *Treatise on the Propagation of Sheep.*

Felicity swallowed a lump of disappointment. She had never believed she could really buy the book, but it had been nice to dream. She pointed out to Elizabeth that the book was gone.

"I wonder who bought it," Elizabeth said.

"Someone well-to-do, I suppose," Felicity said, trying not to sound too envious. Then she remembered why they had come. "I don't see anyone else in the shop right now. Let's hope Widow Reed can tell us something about the broadside."

Elizabeth followed Felicity inside. Widow Reed was just finishing up with a customer, a woman who wanted to advertise her services as a seamstress in the *Gazette.*

After the woman had paid for the ad and

left the shop, Widow Reed greeted Felicity and Elizabeth. "How fares your mother, Felicity? I know your grandfather's sudden passing has been difficult for her." Felicity's grandfather had died only three months ago.

A surge of sadness for him made Felicity's throat feel tight, so all she could manage to say was, "She's well enough, ma'am."

The widow's eyes lingered on Felicity a moment. Then with a gentle pat on Felicity's hand and a sympathetic smile, she said, "He's well remembered, my dear. Now, what can I do for you young ladies?"

"We've come about this, Mistress Reed." Felicity took the broadside out of her pocket, placed it on the counter, and smoothed out the creases. "Did you happen to see one of these?"

"Someone distributed them all over town on the day of the auction," Elizabeth added.

The widow raised her eyebrows. "Ah, yes, I saw this drivel the first day it appeared—and paid it no mind. I doubt anyone in Williamsburg will take it seriously."

In a fleeting moment, Felicity remembered Mother's mention of the women at the market who'd said they would no longer shop with Father. *They* were certainly taking the broadside seriously. But she didn't want to say that to Widow Reed. Instead Felicity asked the widow if she had any idea who might have printed the broadside.

"We've been trying to figure out who this mysterious Mr. Puller might be," Elizabeth said. "We hoped you could help us."

"I shall certainly be happy to try," Widow Reed said. She eased herself to a stool, picked up the broadside, and studied it, tapping a finger on her lip as she read. With a wry face, she laid the broadside back down on the counter. "In the first place, I can't imagine any of the master printers in town being willing to print such lies about your father, Felicity. He's too respected here.

"In the second place, the workmanship of the print job is completely inferior—blurred ink, poor typesetting and design. If any of us produced work like this for our customers, we'd be out of business in a day."

"So you're saying the broadside wasn't printed in Williamsburg?" Elizabeth asked.

"On the contrary," said Widow Reed. "It probably *was* printed here. See? Look at the watermark on this paper. Very distinctive. This paper came from Ramsey's paper mill. Yet I know Alexander Ramsey would never let such poor work past his expert eye."

Slowly she wagged her head. "'Tis a mystery, I'll grant. And one I've been pondering myself since the broadside appeared. I'm sorry I couldn't be of more help, girls. I'd like nothing better than to find the person who would write such things about your father, Felicity."

The girls thanked her, left the shop, and started up the street. The sun had come out from behind some clouds and was already high overhead. "Well," Elizabeth said, "I confess I'm even more baffled about the broadside than I was before. It seemed to me that Widow

Reed was talking in riddles. No one in Williamsburg would print it, she said, yet she was certain it was printed here. How can both be true?"

"They can't," Felicity admitted. She stopped to take off her cloak and throw it over her arm. "One of the Williamsburg printers *has* to have printed the broadside. And I think it was Mr. Ramsey. After all, the broadside was printed on paper from his mill. And—" Felicity hesitated but then told Elizabeth about the letter for Father that had been tampered with at Ramsey's post office.

"But why would Mr. Ramsey do such things?" Elizabeth asked.

"Perhaps Mr. Ramsey thought to drive Father out of business so that he could buy Father's store as cheaply as he bought the McLeods' house," Felicity said.

"'Tis possible," Elizabeth agreed. "Though I wonder what use Mr. Ramsey would have for your father's store. He's a printer, not a storekeeper."

A servant girl sweeping the steps of a house looked up at Felicity and Elizabeth, and the two of them gave her a friendly nod as they passed.

"Mr. Ramsey could sell the store in hopes of making a profit on it," Felicity suggested to Elizabeth. Father *had* said that Ramsey needed money.

"Perhaps," said Elizabeth. "But if he was interested in buying a store cheaply, why didn't he bid on Mr. McLeod's store, the same way Mr. Capps and Mr. Sutherland did? In fact, maybe one of *them* is Mr. Puller. Did you think of that? They're both storekeepers themselves, so they would benefit more than anyone else if your father's store had to close."

Felicity stopped. *"Elizabeth!* You may have something." She told Elizabeth about Father's and Mr. Sutherland's rivalry as young men to marry Mother. "I wonder if Mr. Sutherland has carried a grudge against Father all these years—"

"And is using the broadsides to finally

get even with him." Elizabeth's voice rose in excitement. "Felicity, it makes sense!"

Two women looking in a store window turned and stared at Elizabeth, making her blush. Felicity caught Elizabeth's arm and started walking again. "But that brings us back to the same problem, Elizabeth. Someone would have had to print the broadside *for* Mr. Sutherland. I wonder, though—"

A wagon clattered by in the street, cutting off Felicity's words. When it had passed, Elizabeth asked, "You wonder what?"

Felicity chose her words carefully. "Mr. Sutherland seems to have plenty of money. Both times I've seen him, he was wearing expensive clothes, and at the auction he had on a very fancy wig. He had no trouble outbidding Mr. Capps for Mr. McLeod's store, and Father said he's always made a success of what he's done..."

"Go on," Elizabeth encouraged.

"Well," Felicity started again, "if Mr. Sutherland *has* as much money as I think he does, and Mr. Ramsey *needs* money as badly as *he* seems to . . . maybe Mr. Ramsey was willing to print the broadside because Mr. Sutherland offered him so much money to do it."

"Yes," Elizabeth agreed. "And maybe Mr. Sutherland offered Mr. Ramsey even *more* money to let him read your father's mail. Oh, Felicity, if only we could read the letter of your father's that was opened! It might give us a clue as to whether we're right about Mr. Sutherland, and whether he might be planning something else to hurt your father."

"I would have to go through Father's desk." Felicity's steps slowed. "I hate the thought of it, but I don't see any other way to find out what we need to know. And it is, after all, to help Father."

At that moment, the girls turned the corner and came in view of Merriman's Store. Two men were walking out of the store with Father. "Father's home!" Felicity said happily. But what she saw next made her heart drop to her feet.

TROUBLE FOR FATHER

One of the men pushed Father toward a wagon waiting on the street. The man shoved Father harder, and Father stumbled forward. Then Felicity saw that Father's hands were tied behind him, and she went cold.

Father was being arrested!

7
JAILED!

For one sick moment, Felicity felt glued to the spot, watching as Father climbed into the wagon bed and the two men mounted to the driver's seat. With a "Giddap!" from one of the men to the horse, the wagon lurched forward.

Felicity and Elizabeth exchanged frantic glances and then snatched up their skirts and pitched themselves into a run, past the milliner's shop, past the blacksmith's, past Miss Manderly's house.

Felicity's heart thumped wildly. Her tight bodice squeezed her lungs, and her stays cut into her chest, yet her only thought was to catch up with Father in that wagon. And then she would ... what? She had no idea. But she soon saw that it didn't matter. The wagon had turned the corner and was out of sight.

Felicity stopped in front of the store, her breath coming in heaving gasps. Elizabeth, panting, came up beside her. When Felicity could talk, she said, "Elizabeth, I think they're taking Father to jail!"

"Why on earth, Felicity? What could your father have done?"

The words stung Felicity like a bee. "Nothing! Father would never do anything illegal. There must be some mistake, and I'm going to find out what it is!"

She flew up the steps and into the store, with Elizabeth at her heels. Ben and Marcus were standing just inside the doorway. The skin on Marcus's dark face was stretched tight, and Ben was as pale as his linen shirt.

"Ben! Marcus!" Felicity exclaimed. "What's happened? Who were those two men taking Father away?"

Lines of tension creased the corners of Marcus's mouth. "Your father's been arrested,

Miss Felicity," he said quietly.

"By two men from the Committee of Safety," Ben added in a grieved voice. "They came in here about an hour ago and asked to search the store and go through your father's account books."

A wave of nausea swept over Felicity, and her knees felt loose and wobbly. "Why?" she choked out. Felicity was aware of Elizabeth beside her, heard Elizabeth's deep breathing, felt Elizabeth's light touch on her arm.

Marcus glanced uneasily at Ben, as if he thought it was Ben's place, not his, to answer Felicity's question. "If you'll excuse me," Marcus said, "I have some work to do in the back." With his shoulders slumped, he walked away and disappeared into the back room. Ben stood stiffly, staring after Marcus.

"Ben?" Felicity asked desperately. "Tell me, please. What did the men accuse Father of doing?"

Ben heaved a huge sigh. When he spoke, his voice was weary. "They said your father had made a secret trip to Portsmouth to set up a deal . . . to sell supplies to the British army. To Lord Dunmore's soldiers."

Elizabeth gasped. "That's ridiculous!" Felicity cried.

Ben looked straight at Felicity. "One of the other committee members saw him there, Lissie. In a tavern, meeting with one of Dunmore's officers. He overheard the whole conversation."

"I don't believe it," Felicity said. "It's a mistake! It must've been someone who looked like Father."

"I thought it was a mistake, too," Ben said. "I kept waiting for your father to deny what the men were saying and send them away, but he didn't. Instead, he gave them permission to search the store." His voice had gone dull.

Felicity knew how much Ben admired Father and how his arrest must have shaken Ben. Yet something in Ben's tone made Felicity angry. It was as if Ben believed that Father had done something wrong.

"He let them search because he had nothing to fear, Ben!" she said hotly. "He knew they wouldn't find a thing to support such outrageous charges if they searched the store from top to bottom."

"But they did find something," Ben said miserably. In that same dull voice, he told her: in Mr. Merriman's ledger, the men discovered an entry recording the sale of a large number of goods to an unnamed person in Portsmouth, and in a drawer in his desk they found a receipt for the same goods signed by Lord Dunmore's provision officer. The receipt named Mr. Merriman as the seller of the goods and mentioned payment in gold sovereigns—British coins.

Felicity stood motionless, barely able to breathe. She couldn't believe what Ben was telling her. Elizabeth must have been equally shocked. Her eyes were wide, and her face had paled.

Finally Felicity found her voice. "That's impossible, Ben. Wouldn't you have seen that receipt in his drawer when you went through Father's desk searching for the ledger?"

"Yes, I would've seen it—if it had been there then. But the man showed me the receipt. It was dated three days ago, while your father was away on his business trip. He must have put the receipt in his drawer when he got back from the trip. And Felicity, your father admitted that he went to Portsmouth. But he wouldn't say why."

Felicity seemed to be hearing Ben speak from some faraway place, his words so thin and distant that they couldn't be true. Then slowly, they came drifting toward her, seeping into her brain like a terrible poison.

The blood pounded in her temples. *Father had said he would find a way to pay his debt to Mr. Ramsey. And then he'd abruptly left town on pressing business. Had Father's business been to sell supplies to the British army?*

"No," she said aloud. "I don't believe it!" Then she looked at Ben, at the set of his jaw, the tight line of his lips, and she saw that Ben doubted Father. "Ben, you can't believe that Father is guilty!"

"I don't want to believe it, Felicity," Ben said. "But why wouldn't he explain what he was doing in Portsmouth?"

Suddenly tears were gathering and pressing at Felicity's eyes. *Why, indeed?* she thought. *Why wouldn't Father explain?*

The rest of the day was a blur to Felicity. She moved through it all, watched it all, as if it were happening to someone else: Ben telling Mother of Father's arrest, then Mother telling Nan. William, too young to understand, being told only that Father was away. Mother sending Ben to the jail with food and fresh clothes for Father. All of them sitting through a cheerless supper; Felicity forcing herself to eat, putting food into her mouth that tasted like ashes. Undressing for bed, lying between cold sheets, waiting for sleep that wouldn't come.

She lay in the darkness, listening to the stillness of the night, the creak of the house settling, the scuttling of mice behind the walls, wind outside rattling the branches. Her thoughts twisted like wool on a spinning wheel: *Father in jail ... a receipt for goods sold to Dunmore's soldiers ... a mysterious business trip ... Father's mail tampered with ... Mr. Puller's broadsides ...*

Could all the threads be connected? They must be. But how? And where to begin to piece them all together?

Father's letter.

In the turmoil of the day's events, she'd forgotten all about it. Now the desperate need to read the letter pressed upon her even harder than before. She slipped out of bed and, without bothering with her dressing gown, she hurried down the stairs to the parlor.

In the fireplace a few coals glowed feebly. From the coals Felicity lit a candle and gazed around the room. The comfortable chairs and sofa, Father's mahogany desk in the corner, the figurines and candlesticks on the mantel and the portrait of Grandfather above—they were all so familiar by day, but now, in the heavy darkness, they seemed alien and strange.

Cupping the candle's flame with her hand, she crept to the desk and tried to pull open the lid. It was locked! Disappointment flooded over her. When had Father started locking his desk? Felicity had never seen Father lock the desk, not once. There had to be something very secret in the desk now, something Father wouldn't risk anyone seeing.

What was it?

Felicity's heart thudded. Should she try to find the key to the desk? Did she really want to know what secret Father had locked away inside? If the desk held proof of his innocence, wouldn't he have told someone? The tall clock in the hallway ticked away the minutes while she debated with herself.

At last Felicity dropped her hand from the lid of the desk. It felt too much like betrayal to try to open it when Father obviously wanted to conceal what was inside. And it didn't matter anyway, since she had no idea where he would keep the key. Whatever Father's secret was, she decided, would have to remain just that— his secret. For now at least.

She would have to begin somewhere else, and the most logical starting point was Mr. Puller. Whether he was Mr. Sutherland, Mr. Ramsey, or someone else, Felicity felt sure that he was behind everything, even Father's arrest. If she could discover Mr. Puller's true identity, she believed she would be well on the way toward freeing Father.

Felicity blew out the candle. She padded across the parlor's bare floor, out into the hall-way, and up the stairs. Her mind was already turning, forming a plan to trap Mr. Puller.

With Mr. Puller, all Father's troubles had started, and with Mr. Puller, Felicity determined, Father's troubles were going to end.

8
A TRAP FOR MR. PULLER

In the morning after breakfast, Felicity and
Nan helped Mother make up a basket of food
for Ben to take to Father. In it they put corn
pone and smoked ham from breakfast, a loaf
of crusty bread, a jar of pickles, fruit tarts, and
a jug of cider made from their own apples.
Ben was to take the basket to the jail before he
went to open the store. Mother also wanted
him to find out if Father had been told when
he would stand trial.

Felicity begged Mother to let her go with
Ben to visit Father.

"A jail is no place for a young lady, Felicity,"
Mother said.

Felicity's mind flashed back to last winter,
when Penny's former owner, Jiggy Nye, had

been in jail. Father had sent Felicity and Elizabeth to make a delivery to the jailer, Mr. Pelham, and the girls had chanced to see inside Jiggy Nye's cell. It was small and dank, with only a dim light struggling through the tiny barred window, and nothing but straw on the floor for the prisoners to sleep upon.

A cold shiver ran down Felicity's back. She couldn't bear to think of Father in such a place. And, she thought with sadness, Father probably wouldn't want her to see him there either.

Still, she longed to see Father, if only to catch a glimpse of his face through the window. "Might I at least go with Ben," Felicity asked, "if I promise to wait outside the jail?"

Mother consented, so Felicity set off with Ben. They went up Centre Lane and all the way down Nicholson Street, almost out of town, to where the redbrick jail sat atop a grassy knoll. Across Nicholson Street, the Capitol gleamed brilliant red in the warm morning sunshine. Hundreds of daffodils bloomed along the winding path leading up to the jail, the flowers' bright yellow heads nodding in the breeze. What a contrast, Felicity thought, to the dark, airless cells inside. She hoped Father could look out his window and see the sunny daffodils.

"Why don't you wait there," Ben said, gesturing to a boulder in the shade of some pine trees. "I'll ask your father to wave to you from the window."

Felicity panicked. Did she really want to see Father's dear face behind thick bars of iron? "No, Ben," she stammered. "I've changed my mind. Just tell Father I'm here, and my thoughts are with him."

Ben gave a sad smile. "I'll do that, Lissie."

Felicity watched Ben, carrying the basket, trudge up to the jail's heavy wooden door and knock, and then, when Mr. Pelham opened the door, disappear inside.

When Ben finally returned, all Felicity could bear to ask him was whether Father seemed well.

"Well enough under the circumstances," Ben replied. "I could tell he was hungry, though he invited the other prisoners in the cell to share the food I'd brought." Felicity knew that the only food the jail provided for prisoners was damaged salt beef and coarsely ground meal. Suddenly she wished she and Mother had packed much more in the basket.

"He sends his love to all of you," Ben added. "And he says his trial will be held on Monday."

Even though Father's message made pain twist inside Felicity, her brain began to work. Today was Wednesday; Father's trial was on Monday. That gave her less than a week to carry out her plan.

In her mind, Felicity counted off everything she had to do to set the plan in motion. The first thing was to go to Widow Reed's and place an advertisement in the *Gazette*. She hoped it was not too late to get her advertisement in tomorrow's newspaper. If she shared her plan with Widow Reed, Felicity was sure the widow would do everything she could to bring it about. And, of course, Felicity would have to go to Elizabeth's and get her to help with the rest of the plan.

So much to do and so little time!

Well, today's the day, Felicity said to herself as she got ready for her Friday lessons. She laid her hairbrush on her dressing table and checked her reflection in the swing glass. As usual, a few strands of her stubborn red hair insisted on standing up straight rather than lying in place as they were supposed to, no matter how much brushing she did.

But today it didn't matter. It was so windy that as soon as Felicity stepped outside to go to her lessons, her hair would all fly out of her cap anyway. And she had more important things to think about today than her hair.

She picked up yesterday's *Gazette* from her dressing table and reread, for at least the

tenth time, the advertisement on the bottom
of page four:

> *MR. PULLER!*
> *Your NOTABLE efforts on behalf of the*
> *Patriot cause have come to our attention.*
> *Because you are a SINGULAR PATRIOT,*
> *we have information that will be of great*
> *interest to you. Please inquire for our*
> *letter at Reed's Print Shop before noon on*
> *April 12th.*

Felicity drew a deep breath and released
it slowly. Her stomach felt fluttery. At this
very moment Mr. Puller could be walking into
Widow Reed's shop to pick up the letter she
and Elizabeth had left for him.

In her mind's eye, Felicity pictured the
scene: The book-selling counter of Widow
Reed's shop with its shelves for books and the
mail rack behind. A man's voice asking for a
letter addressed "to a singular Patriot." The
widow's gnarled hand reaching into a slot of

the mail rack and pulling out the letter Felicity
and Elizabeth had so painstakingly written.
The widow passing it to the man and him
taking it. Felicity could almost see his ruffled
shirtsleeve, the fancy cuff of his coat.

She imagined the way he would tuck the
letter into his waistcoat pocket and stride from
the shop in silver-buckled shoes, the way he
would stand on the busy street outside reading
it while passersby hurried past him, the way
he would smile with glee at the offer of "information of great interest to him" that the letter
promised.

Felicity put the newspaper back down on
the table, her heart pounding like a blacksmith's
hammer. She knew the scene wouldn't happen
exactly as she imagined it. But if it happened
at all—if Mr. Puller *did* come for the letter, if
he *did* read it, if the offer of important information *did* appeal to him (and from what Felicity
knew of him, she felt sure it would)—then
Mr. Puller, whoever he was, would come to the
cemetery of Bruton Parish Church tonight at

midnight for a secret meeting with someone
in a blue coat.

And Felicity and Elizabeth just might be
waiting for him there.

After lessons, Felicity and Elizabeth headed
for Widow Reed's print shop to see whether
Mr. Puller had come yet for the letter. The day
was bright and sunny, with fluffy clouds racing
across a brilliant sky. The girls each had to hold
a hand on their straw hats to keep the wind
from lifting the hats right off their heads.

Felicity confessed to Elizabeth that she was
nervous about what they might find out at
Widow Reed's—or even what they might *not*
find out. For, as Widow Reed had pointed out
to them when she'd agreed to help them, there
was no guarantee that Mr. Puller would show
up at all to claim the letter, or that he wouldn't
send a servant to claim it for him.

That's why the girls had set up the meeting

in the cemetery. The meeting was a kind of insurance—scary but necessary—that they would have a chance to spy on Mr. Puller, even if he sent someone else to pick up the letter from Widow Reed's shop.

Elizabeth admitted that she was nervous, too. "I'm more than nervous, to be truthful. I'm *frightened*. What if Mr. Puller isn't Mr. Sutherland *or* Mr. Ramsey? What if he's some-one we don't know—someone *dangerous?* And us alone with him in the cemetery at night! Oh, Felicity, I wish we'd never written that letter at all!"

Felicity wanted to reassure Elizabeth, even though, deep down, she was more than a little frightened herself. "If all goes according to plan, Elizabeth, he'll never see us. We'll be hiding behind gravestones, just close enough to get a look at his face. He'll wait for a while for the blue-coated friend that we mentioned in the letter, and when nobody shows up, he'll leave. And we won't go home till he's long gone. So you see, there's nothing at all to worry about."

Elizabeth stopped and stared at Felicity with saucer eyes. "And what if all *doesn't* go according to plan, Felicity? What then?"

"Well," Felicity said tightly, "*then* we'll worry."

9

MIDNIGHT IN THE CEMETERY

When Felicity and Elizabeth entered Widow Reed's shop, the widow's son, Aaron, was sitting on a stool at the front counter, immersed in a book. A half-eaten apple lay beside the book. Elizabeth asked Aaron if his mother was available. Without looking up, he yelled, "Ma! Customers!"

Widow Reed came out from the back room, wiping ink-stained hands on her apron. "Aaron!" she scolded. "Have a care for your manners. Why don't you go read in back, son?" Aaron nodded, snatched up his apple, and fled.

With a sigh, the widow shook her head. "I apologize for Aaron. He's not so much rude as he is distracted. But I have some distressing news for you, and I'm afraid Aaron is to blame."

She told them that Aaron had given their letter for Mr. Puller to a young boy who'd come for it. The boy said a man off the street had paid him to fetch the letter. The boy had left before Widow Reed could question him about who had sent him. "I'm sorry, girls. I suppose now we'll never know who Mr. Puller really is."

Felicity and Elizabeth exchanged a guilty glance. They had misled Widow Reed about what they'd written in the letter. They had given her the impression that the letter was only a tricky way of making Mr. Puller show himself. They hadn't told her anything about the secret meeting in the cemetery. The widow never would have agreed to help them, Felicity felt sure, if she'd known what they were really planning.

The girls thanked Widow Reed and left the print shop. The late-afternoon sun hung low in the branches of the pecan trees in an orchard across the street. A chilly wind was blowing now, and the clouds that scudded across the sky had turned dark.

As Felicity pulled her cloak tighter against the wind, a strange excitement gripped her. Even though he had sent someone else for the letter, Mr. Puller himself would have the letter in his hands by now; he would have read it. Which meant he would surely show up at the cemetery tonight. What's more, Felicity felt almost certain now that Mr. Puller had to be either Mr. Ramsey or Mr. Sutherland.

"Don't you see?" Felicity said, trying to explain her certainty to Elizabeth. "Mr. Puller must be someone known to Widow Reed, or else he would have come himself for the letter. It fits in perfectly with all the other clues we've figured out."

"At the very least," Elizabeth said, "we know that Mr. Puller is someone we might recognize when we see him tonight. But doesn't that mean he might recognize us, too, if he happens to see us?"

Felicity had already considered that possibility. "That's why we'll be in disguise, Elizabeth. We'll dress like boys, in Ben's breeches. I'm sure he'll lend us each a pair, if I tell him it's part of a scheme to help Father get out of jail."

"Yes," Elizabeth said, smiling, "Ben is certainly accustomed to your schemes."

That night, Felicity, wearing an old pair of Ben's breeches and a heavy cloak, slipped out of the house well before midnight and made her way down Duke of Gloucester Street toward the church. The night was dark and starless. Lanterns burning in front of Chowning's and Market Square taverns gave a dim light that outlined the street.

Felicity passed the courthouse and the Magazine, where muskets and gunpowder were stored. To her right was the Palace Green, stretching like a shadowy carpet to the palace; a lantern gleamed from the cupola on its roof. Just beyond loomed the dark bulk of Bruton Parish Church, its pointed spire rising to a black sky and its white shutters gleaming like rows of teeth. A lighted lantern hung over the door, and in the shadows nearby she saw Elizabeth, also wearing breeches and a cloak, waiting for her.

Together the girls slipped around the church to the walled cemetery. Clouds rolled like smoke over the moon. "'Tis a night fit to be in a graveyard," Felicity said grimly. "Black as a tomb."

The girls huddled behind tall grave-stones near the gate and watched for Mr. Puller. Time dragged. Branches rattled in a rising wind that brought the low growl of distant thunder. Soon a cold, drizzly rain began to fall. Scattered raindrops dripped through the trees and fell to the ground, making an eerie *pat-pat-pat* like the tapping of a cane. The thunder grew closer. Still no Mr. Puller.

Then, somewhere outside the wall, the girls heard the scrape of heavy boots. A man in a billowing cape ducked through the gate, pushing it open with his cane. For an instant, jagged lightning brightened the sky, and Felicity saw a tricornered hat, a large full wig, a face in shadows. Then darkness fell again, and thunder rolled, louder, nearer.

For a long while the man stood at the gate, slowly turning his head, surveying the black churchyard. Felicity's heart thumped in her chest. She willed him to come closer, prayed for another blaze of lightning to reveal his face. He took a few cautious steps forward, toward the stones where Felicity and Elizabeth huddled. Felicity held her breath. Then he stopped, turned around, and stared in the other direction, back toward the church.

What is he doing? Is he going to leave?

He couldn't! Not before she got a good look at him. Felicity leaned toward Elizabeth. "Quick!" she murmured. "We've got to move closer, while his back is turned. Over there."

Felicity nodded toward a pair of tombstones
a few feet nearer the gate.

"We dare not!" Elizabeth whispered back.

"I have to see his face," Felicity insisted.
"'Tis my last chance to help Father!"

With a bob of her chin, Elizabeth consented.
The girls darted toward the gravestones. Then
Felicity felt her foot hit a root. She stumbled,
thudded hard to the ground, lay stunned and
gasping for breath. In a flash of lightning,
Felicity saw the man whirl and raise his cane.
"You, boys! Thieves!" she heard him yell.

Then came a great peal of thunder, and the
man rushed toward her as the heavens opened
and rain poured from the sky.

10

MR. PULLER'S MISTAKE

Everything then happened fast, though it all seemed to Felicity to last a lifetime. Elizabeth was behind her, pulling Felicity up, pushing her forward to run. But the man was already upon them. He caught hold of Felicity, his grasp like a wolf's jaw on her arm. Felicity cried out in fear. "This'll teach you, scoundrel!" the man bellowed, and he raised his cane to deliver a blow.

Rage shot through Felicity. She struggled wildly to break away, flailing and kicking and pummeling the man with her fists. His hat went sailing off his head. Then Felicity heard a *thunk.* The man yelped and buckled, and his cane clattered to the ground. Felicity pulled free from his hold and saw Elizabeth with a branch in hand, her face stark white in the gloom.

"Run!" Elizabeth cried, tossing the branch away. The girls scrambled for the gate as bursts of lightning lit the sky, thunder cracked, and rain beat down in sheets. Out the gate they bolted and up the dark street. Rain lashed their faces; their feet slipped and slid in puddles. Driven by fear, they ran past the Palace Green, past dark houses, not daring to look back.

Finally Felicity risked a glance over her shoulder. She saw nothing behind them but the driving rain. She grabbed Elizabeth's arm to stop her. Felicity's breath came in ragged gulps. "He's not . . . following us," she managed. Elizabeth, gasping for breath, only shook her head in acknowledgment.

"Come on," Felicity said, motioning Elizabeth toward the courthouse across the street. They ducked under the courthouse eaves and huddled there, dripping wet and panting. A stitch in Felicity's side made every breath hurt. When their breathing had slowed, Elizabeth asked Felicity if she was all right.

"I think so," Felicity said, "thanks to you. You were so brave, Elizabeth!"

"He made me so angry," Elizabeth said fiercely, "I didn't even think." Then, shaking her head, she added, "I can't believe I actually *hit* him with a branch. I've never struck anyone in my life."

Felicity gave Elizabeth a reassuring touch. "'Tis a good thing you did. Who knows what he would've done to me—to both of us—if you hadn't stopped him."

"Aye," Elizabeth said. "A pity, though, that we never got a look at his face. Now we'll never know who he was."

"Well, I know who he's *not*," Felicity said. "Mr. Ramsey. A Scotsman like Ramsey would've called us *lads*, not *boys*."

Elizabeth seized on her remark. "You're right! That's something, then. We can rule out Mr. Ramsey." She paused. "I don't suppose you recognized Mr. Puller's voice at all? Did it *sound* like Mr. Sutherland?"

"Maybe," Felicity said uncertainly. "His

voice did seem familiar somehow . . . Oh, I just don't *know,* Elizabeth!" She clenched her fists in frustration. "Everything happened so fast. How I wish I'd gotten a closer look at him!"

"Yes," Elizabeth said, "so do I. But since neither of us did, I suppose all we've learned is who he's *not*—and that isn't much help."

Felicity didn't reply, so discouraging was the thought. For a moment they stood in miserable silence, staring at the rain beating down and splashing off the brick walkway in front of the courthouse. Water from their dripping clothes was making a puddle beneath them, and they were both starting to shiver.

"I suppose we should go home," Elizabeth said, her teeth chattering.

Felicity nodded. She felt wretched about giving up, but what else was there to do?

Suddenly a new thought struck her. "Mr. Puller's cane and hat! He dropped them during the scuffle—"

"Yes!" Elizabeth caught on immediately. "That's probably why he stopped chasing us—

to go back and look for them."

"But he may not be able to find them in the dark, Elizabeth, and I should think he wouldn't dare look for them in daylight—"

"So if we go back to the churchyard tomorrow, we might find them!"

"Aye," Felicity said, her spirits rising. "That would at least give us some clue to go on."

After agreeing to meet in the churchyard after breakfast, the girls said good-bye and made their separate ways home. The rain had let up and was only a drizzle by the time Felicity reached her house. She crept up the back stairs and slipped out of her wet clothes and into a dry night-shift. She climbed into bed, and before she knew it, she was asleep.

The next morning was clear and bright. The night's storm had swept the sky clean of clouds, and the sun was warm even under the great trees in the churchyard. Felicity and

Elizabeth searched the cemetery from one
end to the other for Mr. Puller's hat and cane,
among all the tombstones and even under the
hedge along the churchyard wall, but they
found nothing. "Likely he came back to retrieve
them at first light," Elizabeth guessed.

Felicity nodded her agreement, but she
didn't answer. She was thinking hard about
something else: Mr. Puller's wig. In the flash
of lightning when Mr. Puller had first come
through the gate, Felicity had noticed his
large wig.

Today, while she and Elizabeth had been
searching for the hat and cane, Felicity had
been mulling over that wig. She was almost
sure it was a bob wig, like the one Grandfather
had sometimes worn on special occasions. Bob
wigs had fluffy curls and were somewhat out
of fashion. Most younger men in Williamsburg
wore smaller, more stylish wigs or didn't wear
wigs at all.

She recounted her thinking for Elizabeth
and added, "On the day of the auction, I

remember, Mr. Sutherland was wearing a rather large wig."

"A bob wig?"

"It might have been," Felicity said, "though I'm not certain. But, Elizabeth, what I'm getting at is this: Mr. Puller's wig would've gotten soaked last night in the rain and lost its shape."

Which meant, she went on, that he would have to take it to a wigmaker's shop to be repaired. And that meant she and Elizabeth could visit the wigmakers' shops in Williamsburg to see who had brought in such a wig for repair. "And then we'll have our man!" she finished.

Tingling with excitement, the girls decided to start their search with George Lafong's shop, since it was the busiest wigmaker's establishment in Williamsburg. It stood at the other end of Duke of Gloucester Street, near the Capitol and next door to the King's Arms Tavern.

When they got there, the shop was bustling. Felicity let her eyes roam the room. Several men and a woman were busy making wigs, and another man in front of a window was dusting a customer's hair with powder. One gentleman sat in a barber chair getting a shave, and Mr. Lafong was talking with a customer at a table, showing him various styles of wigs.

Then, in a corner of the room, Felicity saw what she was looking for: two bob wigs being dressed and curled by an apprentice. Her heart beat a little faster as she pointed out the wigs to Elizabeth.

"Let's go talk to him," Elizabeth suggested. "We could pretend to have an interest in ordering something from the shop, a pair of curls or some such. Perhaps we can get him to tell us something about the wigs."

Felicity nodded. Pretending to look at the various hairpieces on display, the girls wandered over to the apprentice and struck up a conversation with him. The young man was talkative, and, with a little flattery for his skill, the girls had no trouble turning the conversation to the wigs he was working on. "I suppose you do most of the wig repairs," Felicity commented.

"Aye, that I do," the young man replied.

"Then you must be very good, and very quick," Elizabeth added. "These wigs look as if they're nearly finished. Were they brought in only this morning for repair?"

"Indeed, they were," he said, squaring his shoulders with pride. "By two very distinguished gentlemen, I might add, leaders in our city's government. You may understand why I'm honored that my master trusts me with such important work."

A leader in the government? Felicity couldn't imagine any government official being as despicable as Mr. Puller.

Bitterly disappointed, Felicity glanced at Elizabeth, who sadly shook her head. "We must be going," Felicity told the apprentice, and the girls started to leave. At the door, Felicity stopped and stared.

There in the umbrella stand was a fancy cane with a silver boar's head on top. Suddenly

Felicity's heart was pounding. She knew she had seen the cane before—in Father's store on the day Fiona showed Felicity and Elizabeth the broadside against Fiona's father.

There couldn't be another cane like it in all of Williamsburg.

11

FATHER'S SECRET

Felicity rushed back to the apprentice. "If you please," she said, "could you tell me the names of the two gentlemen whose wigs you're working on?"

Puffing himself up, the apprentice replied, "One is Mr. John Randolph, our attorney general, and the other is Mr. Richard Capps, a member of our Committee of Safety. As I said, both are important men in Williamsburg."

Felicity felt a pressure growing in her chest so that she could hardly speak. "I believe Mr. Capps has left his cane," she stammered, pointing to the umbrella stand.

The apprentice glanced at the stand. "Oh, my word, he has. He'll be back, I'm certain, to claim it. Likely 'tis worth a great deal."

Blood was thundering through Felicity's head. She clenched Elizabeth's arm and pulled her out of the shop. The minute they were outside, she said breathlessly, "Elizabeth! I know who Mr. Puller is!"

Elizabeth's eyes went wide with astonishment.

"It's Mr. Capps," Felicity said. "It must be!" Quickly she explained, while knots of people passed them on the sidewalk. First there was the wig, she told Elizabeth. Then there was the fact that Capps owed Mr. McLeod money, which he wouldn't—or couldn't—pay.

"I think Mr. Capps's business must be in trouble," Felicity said. "His apprentice, Walter, is a friend of Ben's, and Walter told us Mr. Capps's store isn't doing very well. I think Capps saw a chance to put Fiona's father out of business and maybe get his store cheaply at the same time. And Capps was angry with Mr. McLeod anyway. Remember? Mr. McLeod said they'd had an argument."

Elizabeth was nodding, so Felicity rushed

on. As a member of the Committee of Safety, Felicity pointed out, Capps could easily bring accusations of disloyalty against Mr. McLeod— and some on the committee would be eager to believe the accusations just because Mr. McLeod was Scottish. "And when Father stood up for Mr. McLeod, Capps must have gotten the idea to do the same thing to Father."

"It makes perfect sense!" Elizabeth said. "Mr. Capps's store was failing, and your father's and Mr. McLeod's stores were doing well."

Felicity stepped aside to let two men go into the wig maker's. "Only the way it worked out, Capps *wasn't* able to buy Mr. McLeod's store because Mr. Sutherland outbid him."

"Making Capps all the more determined to get your father's store," Elizabeth agreed. Then she drew down her brows, thinking hard. "But Mr. Capps isn't a printer. Who would have printed the broadsides for him?"

Felicity chewed on her lip, considering. "Walter said Capps always seemed to have gold coins to spend, even though the store wasn't making much money. Maybe Capps used some of that gold to convince Mr. Ramsey to print the broadside for him."

"Well," Elizabeth said a bit uncertainly, "we never did get a chance to question Mr. Ramsey about the broadsides."

"We could go now," Felicity said, getting excited. "Mr. Ramsey's shop is just down the street."

"I doubt he would tell us the truth, Felicity," Elizabeth said in a sober tone. "Especially since your father was arrested partly as a result of the broadside. If Mr. Ramsey *did* print it and he *truly* respects your father, as Widow Reed said he does, he's certain to be ashamed of what he's done and how it turned out."

"Perhaps *he* won't tell us the truth," Felicity said with determination, "but if we ask the right questions, his apprentice *might*."

Elizabeth smiled. "If it worked once, it might work again. Let's go."

Mr. Ramsey's print shop was three doors down from the wigmaker's. When the girls walked into the print shop, the bell on the front door jangled furiously. But there was no one at the counter, and no one responded to the bell. From the back room, where the printing press was located, came angry shouting in a thick Scottish accent. The door to the back room was open slightly, and Felicity caught sight of a red-faced Ramsey standing over the printing press, shaking his fist at his apprentice, Zachary.

"The devil take you, lad!" Mr. Ramsey was saying. "How often must I tell ye a puller needs to take his time when he's inking the press? Every sheet you've printed is blurred. The entire job must be redone! I canna leave the shop for a moment, can I?"

"Maybe we should leave, Felicity," whispered Elizabeth. "I suspect this isn't a good time to talk to Mr. Ramsey's apprentice."

Felicity only half-heard Elizabeth. She was too focused on Mr. Ramsey's words. *Puller . . . blurred ink . . .* Then Mr. Ramsey said something else, and the final piece of the puzzle clicked into place. "If ye werena Richard Capps's nephew," Ramsey bellowed, "I'd have gotten rid of ye months ago!"

Zachary was Mr. Capps's nephew!

In a flash Felicity knew how Capps had gotten the broadsides printed. Zachary had done it when Mr. Ramsey was out of the shop! And with Mrs. Ramsey sick, that would have been often. Felicity could well imagine Zachary, the puller who operated the press, gleefully signing the broadsides "Mr. Puller," figuring no one would ever realize where the name came from.

Felicity and Elizabeth exchanged glances. They hurried out of the shop and stood on the sidewalk outside, talking about what they'd heard. "'Tis clear as a bell now," Felicity said. "Mr. Capps had Zachary print the broadsides—*and* open Father's mail!"

"What a scoundrel, to use his own nephew in such a fashion!" Elizabeth exclaimed. "What could Capps have learned in that letter, Felicity? Do you think the letter could be behind your father's arrest?"

Felicity stared at Elizabeth. She hadn't even thought of that! But now that Elizabeth had suggested it, she saw how logical it was. Ben had said that someone from the Committee of Safety claimed to have seen Father meeting with a British officer in Portsmouth. And Mr. Capps was on the Committee of Safety. Capps must have learned in the letter he opened that Father was going to Portsmouth on some kind of business. So he lied about seeing Father there with the officer!

Felicity shared her thinking with Elizabeth. "What I *don't* understand," Felicity said, "is why Father didn't stand up for himself. Why didn't he explain what his business in Portsmouth was?"

"Perhaps the answer to that question is in the letter itself," Elizabeth said. "You must find a way to read it, Felicity."

"I've already tried," Felicity said. "Father has locked the desk where he keeps his correspondence—"

"That's what keys are for," Elizabeth broke in. "Where does your father keep the key to the desk? Do you have any idea?"

"No," Felicity replied. Then a new thought came to her. "Wait," she said. "I know where Father keeps *some* of his keys—in a wooden box on the bureau in his bedchamber. Maybe one of those keys fits his desk."

"Is there some way you could sneak into his chamber and look in the box?"

"I could do it now," Felicity said. "Mother was to take coffee at the Whythes' this morning to talk about Father's defense." Mr. Whythe was a lawyer as well as a family friend. "And 'tis market day, so Rose will be out of the house as well."

"I'll help you," Elizabeth said eagerly. "Mother and Annabelle are also out for the morning, so I shan't be missed."

"Perfect," Felicity exclaimed. "Let's go!"

When the girls got to Felicity's house, they checked every room to be certain no one was home. Then Felicity led the way upstairs to her parents' bedchamber. Morning sun through the windows made patchwork patterns on the floor and the crocheted coverlet on the high, curtained bed. Motioning Elizabeth to come with her, Felicity stepped into the room and over to the bureau. "Here's Father's box," she said, gingerly touching the polished wood of the lid.

"'Tis beautiful," Elizabeth murmured. "Go on. Open it."

Carefully Felicity lifted the lid. On the red velvet cloth inside lay a timepiece, a silver snuffbox, and several pieces of jewelry, but no keys.

"Perhaps in the little drawers," Elizabeth offered, pointing to the tiny wooden drawers at the back of the box.

One by one, Felicity slid open the drawers. The first contained a jeweled watch fob, the second was empty, and in the third were two small brass keys. Felicity's heart lifted with excitement. "Well," she said, holding one key in each hand, "let's hope one of these fits the desk."

The girls flew down the stairs to the parlor. Elizabeth kept watch at the window while Felicity tried the keys in the lock of Father's desk. The first key she tried slipped neatly into the keyhole and turned with a *click*. "It fits!"

"Excellent," Elizabeth said. "Now hurry and find the letter."

Felicity took a deep breath and lifted the lid of the desk.

Inside, the desk was neatly organized, with letters and papers tied in labeled bundles. Felicity flipped through the bundles. One bundle was labeled "Commissary business." This was Father's work for the Patriots, helping to locate and deliver supplies to the army. At the top of the bundle, she saw an important-looking letter dated April 2, 1776, almost two weeks ago.

Felicity figured up the days. The timing was right. Was this the letter that had been tampered with? Her heart thumped wildly as her eyes flew over the words.

The letter called Father to Portsmouth to

arrange a deal with a local farmer who had
offered to sell food to the Patriot army. In public the farmer pretended to be a Loyalist, but
he was secretly providing information to the
Patriots about the movements of the British
army. The letter warned that the farmer's identity and details of the deal must be kept secret
at all costs. With Lord Dunmore's ships nearby
in the bay, if word of the farmer's identity were
to leak out, it could put him in great danger.

Felicity's skin prickled. *Father was protecting
a Patriot spy.* That's why he couldn't tell
the reason he'd gone to Portsmouth!

She called Elizabeth over and read the
letter to her. With each word Felicity read
aloud, Mr. Capps's plan to ruin Father became
clearer in her mind. Finally she realized how
Capps had pulled it off. She dropped the letter
into her lap.

"How dull-witted I've been not to see it
sooner," Felicity said. "The receipt from the
British officer that was found in Father's
drawer—Mr. Capps put it there! After he read

this letter, he knew that Father was going to be away in Portsmouth, so he distracted Ben, sneaked into Father's office, and stole the account ledger. That's why Ben couldn't find it anywhere."

"Capps must have altered the ledger to make it *look* as if your father had been selling to the British. Then he returned later to put it back," Elizabeth said.

"Which is when Ben found it again in plain sight." Felicity's voice rose forcefully. "But the most important part is this, Elizabeth: Capps got the idea of accusing Father of selling to the British because Capps is doing it *himself*. That must be how he happened to have a receipt from Lord Dunmore's officer."

Elizabeth looked confused. "How can you be so certain?"

Felicity filled in the rest of the details for Elizabeth: how Walter had told her and Ben about Capps's frequent trips to Portsmouth; how Walter thought Capps was selling to a rich Loyalist there, because Capps always seemed to have British gold to spend.

"British gold," Felicity said with intensity, "that he got from making deals to sell supplies to Dunmore's soldiers." She paused and glanced at Elizabeth to see her reaction.

Elizabeth was frowning and pursing her lips, as if she was thinking hard about what Felicity had said, so Felicity went on. "When Capps told the Committee of Safety that he suspected Father of selling supplies to Dunmore, he knew full well that Father couldn't reveal the *real* reason he'd been in Portsmouth.

"And since the broadside had already put the suspicion into some people's minds that Father was disloyal, some of the members must have believed Capps enough to go to Father's store to investigate his claims." Felicity stopped, her throat suddenly too tight to go on.

"Where they found the receipt and the ledger book that supposedly proved your father was guilty," Elizabeth finished for her. "And since he couldn't tell why he had *really* been to Portsmouth, he couldn't speak up in his own defense. Oh, Felicity!" Elizabeth clasped Felicity's hands in hers. "What an unthinkable predicament for your father to be in!"

Elizabeth's words hung in the air, awful but true. Felicity nodded, too numb to speak—and too afraid. Father was caught in an impossible bind, and it seemed there was no way out. Whatever he did, there would be terrible consequences.

If Father couldn't reveal his true business in Portsmouth without putting the farmer in danger, he couldn't defend himself at his trial. And with Mr. Capps testifying against him, Father would surely be found guilty, and be sentenced to prison—or worse.

12

A DESPERATE SITUATION

A wave of nausea rolled over Felicity. Father's trial was on Monday, the day after tomorrow.

What will happen to him?

Felicity squeezed her lids shut against the tears filling her eyes, slipped her hands from Elizabeth's, and went to the window. She pulled back the damask curtains and stared out at the street. The sun sparkled on windows across the street and flashed off the brass of a fine carriage going by. From an apple tree by the walk, Felicity could hear a cardinal singing, his bright red feathers no match for the brilliant-hued clothes of men and women strolling on the sidewalk.

Felicity swallowed hard. How could the

world outside go on so gaily when her own world was falling apart?

Then she felt Elizabeth's hand on her shoulder, and she turned. Elizabeth was standing beside her. "Oh, Elizabeth," Felicity said, a sob catching in her throat. "I can't bear the thought of what might happen to Father."

Elizabeth hugged Felicity. "Surely there's something we can do to help your father, Felicity. Perhaps we could go to the committee and tell them what we know about Capps—"

Felicity, her voice cracking over tears, said, "They would never believe us. We have no proof that Capps has done anything wrong."

"Well," Elizabeth said uncertainly, as if her thoughts were still forming as she spoke, "if Capps had one receipt from Dunmore's officer—the one he left in your father's desk— wouldn't he, perhaps, have more of them? Walter said that Capps went to Portsmouth often, did he not? So he must have been doing business with Dunmore for a while."

Suddenly Felicity saw what Elizabeth was

getting at, and a dark weight slipped from her mind. "Elizabeth, how clever you are!" she said. With her sleeve Felicity swiped the tears from her cheeks. "All we have to do is get our hands on those other receipts and show them to the committee. With everything else we've found out about Capps, it'll be obvious to the committee that he framed Father."

"Do you think Walter will help us?" Elizabeth asked.

"I know he will," Felicity replied. "Ben says Walter doesn't like Mr. Capps. Let's go talk to Ben."

At the store, Ben was waiting on a man wearing a long, fringed buckskin hunting shirt and buckskin pants. The man wanted to exchange the animal furs he had brought in for tobacco, but Ben seemed reluctant to make the trade. "I'm not sure I can do that without Mr. Merriman here," Ben said.

145

"When will he return?" the man asked. "I'll be in town for a few days."

"He . . . I don't think he'll be back by then." Ben's face was flushed.

Felicity felt like crying. Ben was embarrassed to tell the man where Father really was. What's worse, Felicity couldn't blame him. She felt her own face go red.

Ben glanced at her and Elizabeth. Then he quickly said to the man, "Listen, I'll go ahead and make the trade." Hastily Ben reached for the can of tobacco, measured the tobacco out, wrapped it in paper, and tied it up with string. The man thanked him and strode out of the store.

"I'm sorry, Lissie," Ben said. "I don't know how to explain to customers about your father."

"Don't worry, Ben," Felicity said, trying to keep her voice from shaking. "I understand." Then she and Elizabeth told Ben their reason for coming, explaining to him everything they had figured out about Capps and how they hoped Walter would help them. When they'd finished, Ben's eyes were blazing.

"What a scoundrel!" Ben said. "He must've stolen the ledger that day he had me searching through stacks of merchandise and didn't buy a thing. And he came back the next day and had Marcus and me load his wagon with more bags of rice than a person could use in a year, while he waited inside the store."

"Where he was putting the ledger back and slipping the receipt into Father's drawer," Felicity threw in.

"Aye," Ben said. "I wondered why Capps was doing so much shopping at a competitor's store. We'll fix him, though." He snatched a quill pen from the counter, dipped it in ink, and jotted a note to Walter, asking Walter to meet him and Felicity at the Merrimans' stable that evening. He folded it and handed it to Felicity. "Does Mr. Capps know you, Lissie? If you take this note to Walter, will Capps recognize you?"

"I don't think so," Felicity replied.

"Just the same, try not to let him see you too closely," Ben instructed. "No use making him suspicious. If Capps is there, Elizabeth, you distract him somehow, while Lissie gives the note to Walter."

The girls agreed and then headed to Mr. Capps's store. The store was in a small clapboard building on Blair Street. The only other business nearby was a shoemaker's shop next to the store. The shop's door was open to the warm spring breeze. As the girls passed, they glimpsed the shoemaker sitting astride his benchlike sewing horse. The man saw them looking at him and smiled and waved. The girls waved back.

"He's a friendly sort," Elizabeth remarked.

"Unlike the man we're going to see," Felicity said, dread in her voice. The girls were lingering outside Capps's store underneath its sign depicting a woman holding a shopping basket.

"Perhaps Mr. Capps won't even be here," Elizabeth said hopefully.

"I'm afraid I would never have such good fortune," Felicity said. "Let's get this over with." She started up the steps to the store, and Elizabeth followed her.

Felicity shot Elizabeth an "I told you so" look as they entered. Mr. Capps, clad in a burgundy waistcoat and a fine linen cravat, was at the front counter, writing in his ledger book. One quick glance at the store's scantily stocked shelves confirmed to Felicity that the store didn't have much business. Felicity saw Walter at the back of the store, arranging some boxes. Capps looked up briefly at the girls, but then went back to writing. Felicity imagined that he didn't think two young girls were important enough customers to interrupt his work.

With a quick nod to each other, the girls parted. They had already planned what each of them would do. Elizabeth marched up to the counter, while Felicity sidled back toward Walter. "Please, sir," Elizabeth said to Capps, "do you have fresh ginger today?"

Walter saw Felicity coming down the aisle and started to greet her, but Felicity raised a finger to her lips to quiet him. Walter furrowed his brows in puzzlement, so Felicity pulled the note from her pocket and pointed to it. Silently she mouthed, "It's from Ben," and pressed it into Walter's hand.

Then, wanting Capps to hear her, she said loudly, "If you please, young man, I'd like to look at baskets."

Walter winked at her. He had caught on to what she was doing. He slipped the note into his own pocket and said, "Certainly, young miss." He climbed a ladder nearby, plucked several baskets from the display rope hung from the rafters, and showed them to Felicity.

Felicity pretended to examine the baskets. Then she clicked her tongue. "I don't believe I shall purchase any of these today," she said crisply. She thanked Walter and headed to the front of the store, where Elizabeth was lifting lids and sniffing at several jars of herbs and spices that Capps had pulled from the shelves.

Felicity caught Elizabeth's eye and gave a slight nod. Elizabeth plunked the lid back on top of a jar. "No thank you, sir," she said, turning up her nose. "I don't believe any of these spices will be fresh enough for my mother."

A scowl spread on Capps's face. "You'll find no fresher spices in Williamsburg, young lady," he growled.

With a toss of her head, Elizabeth turned away and said, "I shall try Merriman's." Then she sailed out the door at the same time as Felicity. Outside, the girls couldn't help giggling together at Capps's reaction. "'Twas a brilliant performance you gave," Felicity told Elizabeth. "Capps looked near to having a fit when you insulted his spices."

"I do believe his face was a darker red than his waistcoat," Elizabeth agreed, laughing. "In all seriousness, though," she added, her expression turning sober, "I am right glad to be out of there. There's something about Mr. Capps that makes my flesh creep."

"I know what you mean," Felicity said.

"Almost like having a cockroach scuttle across your foot." The girls burst into giggles again. Then Elizabeth said that she needed to be getting home for the midday meal.

"Oh, yes," Felicity said. "I should be going too. Mother will be home soon, and I promised to mind William and Polly for her."

Elizabeth wished Felicity well in the meeting with Walter. "I'll see you at church tomorrow," she added, "and you can tell me how it went."

That evening, Felicity and Ben waited in the stable for Walter to arrive. It was nearly dusk when Walter finally showed up. He apologized for being so late in coming. "I had to wait until Mr. Capps left the store to go to the tavern for his nightly mug of ale," he said. "What's the matter, Ben?"

Together Ben and Felicity filled Walter in on everything that had happened. When they had finished the story, Walter let out a long, low whistle. "Sounds like trouble enough to make Job swear," he said in dismay. "I've never cared much for Mr. Capps, but—"

"Never cared much for him!" Ben interrupted. "Walter, you detest the man!"

Walter's mouth twitched into the hint of a smile. "True, my friend, true. Yet somehow I never figured him for a traitor."

"It fits with his character, does it not?" Felicity said fiercely.

"Aye," Walter agreed, nodding. "Hypocrite to the core."

Ben narrowed his eyes. "Then you wouldn't mind seeing Capps taken in his own net?"

"Nothing would please me more," Walter said. "A man who trumpets his patriotism with one hand and betrays his countrymen with the other deserves what he gets."

Felicity fixed Walter with a hopeful gaze. "Does that mean you'll help us search for the receipts?"

"Of course," Walter said, "though I don't think we'll need to search very far. Likely

Mr. Capps has them locked up in the strongbox in his office at the store. And I know where he keeps the key."

"Good," Ben said. "Is there any way we can get into the office tomorrow to search, since the store will be closed?"

"Not a chance," Walter said. "Mr. Capps will keep me under his thumb all day. There's church in the morning, and then an endless Sunday dinner with his wife's sister and her unbearable son, Zachary." He grimaced, as if he couldn't stand the thought.

"Couldn't you slip away and unlock the store while everyone's at dinner? Then Ben and I could search the office ourselves," Felicity suggested.

Walter shook his head. "Too risky. Sometimes Mr. Capps skips Sunday dinner with the excuse of catching up on his bookkeeping at the store. *I* think he just wants to avoid Zachary."

"But we must search *sometime* tomorrow!" Felicity said, desperation drying her throat.

"Father's trial is on Monday!"

"We'll do it Monday," Walter said, "while Mr. Capps is at the trial. He told me he's testifying against your father." Walter gave Felicity a sympathetic look, and suddenly her eyes were blurring with tears.

Ben noticed Felicity's distress. "'Tis the best way, Lissie," he said gently, "to be certain Mr. Capps will be gone."

"But that gives us so little time!" Felicity cried. Her voice came out in a croak.

"'Twill have to be time enough," Ben said with intensity, "for it's all we have."

13
TRIAL DAY

Sunday seemed to drag by. When bedtime came, Felicity was relieved that the day was finally over. Tomorrow she could at last do *something* to help Father. She only hoped her help would come in time.

Felicity tossed and turned all night, and in the morning she felt as if she hadn't slept at all. She was glad when she and Ben finally were on their way to meet Walter at Mr. Capps's store on Blair Street. At the end of Duke of Gloucester Street, Felicity could see the red-brick Capitol building. Was Father there inside the courtroom at that very moment, await-ing trial? Dread gnawed at her insides. "Let's hurry, Ben," she said.

Past the Capitol they went. As they turned

the corner onto Blair, they had a clear view of the avenue all the way down to Francis Street: white clapboard houses with white picket fences, the friendly shoemaker's shop, and Mr. Capps's store.

Then Felicity's breath caught in her throat. Mr. Capps was coming out of his store. And he was walking right toward them!

Ben saw Capps at the same time Felicity did. "Quick!" Ben said. "This way!" He pulled Felicity into a narrow path between two high boxwood hedges. There they crouched and waited for Capps to pass. From the other side of the hedge came the sound of squawking ducks and chickens and the barking of a dog.

Fine! Felicity thought. *Just what we need is for some dog to come sniffing at us and give us away to Mr. Capps.*

Then Mr. Capps was walking by. All that Felicity could see was his legs: fine white stockings, silver-buckled shoes, his cane swinging merrily with every step. *And he was whistling.* Felicity was furious. Capps couldn't wait to testify against Father! When he had passed, she said as much to Ben.

"Never mind," Ben said. "His mood will change when he finds *himself* standing trial instead of your father."

Felicity and Ben waited on the path between the hedges until Capps was well across Blair Street. Then they dashed around to the back of Capps's store, where Walter let them in and led them into the office.

"Perfect timing," Walter told them. "Mr. Capps just left."

"I know," Ben said. "We almost ran into him." Then they heard the faint jingling of a bell.

"Confound it!" Walter said. "A customer! I forgot to lock the front door." He eased the office door open to see who was in the store. A stout woman was standing at the counter, holding a basket with a live chicken inside. "'Tis Mrs. Ludwell," Walter said. "I'll try to get rid of her quickly." Before Felicity or Ben could say a word, Walter had ducked out of the office and closed the door behind him.

Felicity gave Ben an exasperated look. "What do we do now, Ben?"

"We wait," Ben replied, seating himself on a barrel. Biting her lip, Felicity sat down on the barrel beside Ben and crossed her ankles. Her stomach had tightened into an icy knot.

It seemed to take forever, but at last Walter returned. "This time I've locked the store," he said. "Now for the key to the strongbox. Mr. Capps keeps it behind a loose board in the wall."

In a few paces he was at the wall, running his hand over the rough boards. "Right about . . . here." He pushed aside a board and reached behind it. When he drew out his hand, he was clutching a brass key. Felicity felt a thrill skip over her nerves.

With an expression of triumph on his face, Walter held the key up for Felicity and Ben to see. "Key found. We're halfway there," he said. "Felicity, the strongbox is on that shelf above you. Bring it down and hand it to me, please."

Her hands shaking, Felicity reached up to the shelf and handed down to Walter a small iron box fastened with a padlock. She watched, stiff with suspense, while Walter fitted the key into the lock and turned it. With a *click,* the padlock fell open.

The next few moments seemed endless as Walter lifted the lid, pulled out a stack of papers, and looked through them. Finally he looked up at Felicity. "The receipts are here," he said. "A whole stack of them. And from the look of the dates on them, Mr. Capps has been supplying Dunmore for months."

With a hiss, Felicity released the breath she didn't know she was holding. Walter handed some of the receipts to Felicity and Ben to examine. Relief pumping through her, Felicity flipped through the receipts, scarcely able to see for the tears in her eyes. "Will these do it, Ben?" she asked hoarsely. "Will these save Father?"

"They're bound to," Ben said, excitement in his voice. "They're exactly like the receipt the committee found in your father's drawer. Same signature, same handwriting, everything. It should be clear to any court in the land that Capps took one of these receipts and altered it to make your father look guilty."

"Then we have to get the receipts to the justices at Father's trial," Felicity said. "Let's get to the courtroom before it's too late!"

With the receipts in hand, Felicity, Ben, and Walter scrambled out of Capps's office and bolted up Blair Street toward the Capitol. At the gate to the Capitol grounds, the boys let Felicity take the lead, and the three of them sprinted up the brick walkway to the Capitol building. Felicity pitched herself up the steps and through the arch. Then she turned left through a short hallway to the chamber of the General Court. At the massive doors she stopped, suddenly afraid.

"Go in," Ben said firmly. "We'll be right behind you."

"Aye," said Walter.

Felicity drew a deep breath and pushed open

the door to the courtroom. In a split second she took it all in—the rich mahogany paneling on the walls, the high U-shaped bench for the justices, their dark robes and their white powdered wigs, Father at the rail opposite the justices' bench, Mr. Whythe beside Father, Mr. Capps a few feet behind them. It was all a jumble, a sweep of color and staring faces, until Felicity's gaze rested on Father. He was unshaven and gaunt and his clothes were disheveled, yet he stood as straight and tall as ever.

Father's eyes flew open with shock at seeing her. "Felicity! What are you doing here?" he cried.

"Father, we have evidence to prove you're innocent!"

Afterward, Felicity could recall only bits and pieces of what had happened in the courtroom: the uproar at her announcement; Mr. Capps, white-faced, with his mouth hanging open; the chief justice calling her and Ben and Walter to the witness stand; Father's hand on her shoulder as she testified; and then the justices conferring to reach a decision.

One thing, though, stood out clearly in Felicity's mind, and she was sure she would remember it forever. In that very long moment after the justices turned back to the courtroom to present their verdict, and the chief justice, in his deep, booming voice, pronounced Father innocent, Father had wrapped Felicity in a hug, and Felicity saw that his eyes were wet with tears. It was all she could do to stop herself from breaking down in sobs. Then she had looked up, and over Father's shoulder, she saw Capps being led away to jail. She couldn't see his face, but she could tell by his bent head and slumped shoulders that his angry, arrogant behavior was at last gone.

Felicity didn't feel sorry for him in the least.

14
A CELEBRATION

At supper that night, Felicity's heart felt full. The dining room glowed in the soft light of hearth and candle. Outside, a gentle spring rain was falling. The delicate cut glass on the chandelier shimmered like so many diamonds, and the windowpanes glistened with rain-drops. Father was at his place at the head of the table, clean and freshly shaven and looking himself again. The rest of the family was there, too, including Ben. Even Baby Polly was asleep in her cradle at Mother's side.

While everyone ate, Felicity told how she, with Elizabeth's, Ben's, and Walter's help, had discovered Mr. Puller's identity and worked to free Father from jail. Nan was listening so hard, she didn't interrupt even once. When

Felicity finished, Nan was wide-eyed. "Weren't you scared in the courtroom, Lissie?" she asked in an awed voice.

"Out of my wits," Felicity said. "But once I began talking about everything Mr. Capps had done to Father, I got angry all over again, and I forgot to be scared."

Mother's lips twitched. "Just as you've forgotten to eat your supper tonight," she teased.

"Oh," Felicity said, looking down with surprise at the scarcely touched food on her plate. She quickly dug into the meaty Brunswick stew Rose had prepared.

"What of your friend Walter?" Mother asked Ben. "What will he do now that Mr. Capps is out of business?" She was trying to wipe sticky jam off William's face, and, as usual, he was trying to squirm away.

Ben spread jam on his fourth biscuit. "Well," he said, a glimmer of mischief in his eyes, "Walter never much liked storekeeping. And being the enterprising fellow that he is, he's already found another job."

"Yes," said Felicity, "he came by and told Ben and me about it this evening."

Father patted his mouth with a linen napkin. He had finished eating and pushed away his plate. "Where will Walter be working?"

"For Mr. Ramsey," Felicity said.

"As soon as Mr. Ramsey found out what had happened to Mr. Capps," Ben said, "he wasted no time in firing Zachary and putting a 'Help Wanted' sign in his window. Walter saw the sign, went in, and promptly got the job. He starts tomorrow."

Mother had finally gotten William's face clean, and now she was finishing up her own supper. "All's well that ends well, then," she said. She looked across the table at Felicity and added, "Though there's no doubt the ending might have been very different, if not for our Lissie's efforts."

Mother's words brought Fiona and her family to Felicity's mind. She hoped the McLeods would find a happy ending in their new home, too.

William had worn a puzzled frown throughout the conversation; he didn't understand most of what was being said. But now the frown disappeared, and his face lit up. "Then Lissie's a hero!" he cried, raising his chubby arms in the air.

"Why, yes," Father said, an amused expression on his face. "Indeed she is. And since we all know that heroes deserve rewards, I have something I'd like to present to Felicity now."

"A reward?" Nan asked eagerly.

Felicity was a little embarrassed. "'Tis reward enough to have you home, Father," she said softly.

"I thank you for that, my dear," Father said. "What I have to give you isn't really a reward, though it is something you deserve." He glanced at Mother, and she gave an approving smile. Father's eyes were twinkling when he spoke again. "I know your birthday is yet a few days away, Lissie, but I think this a fitting occasion for you to receive the gift your mother and I have for you."

"We'd been planning to give you something special to acknowledge the fine young gentle-woman you're becoming," Mother added.

A birthday present. With all that had happened lately, Felicity had forgotten all about her birthday.

Father reached under the tablecloth for something he must have had in his lap. When he brought out his hand, he was holding a book, and not just any book—it was the leather-bound copy of *Gulliver's Travels* from Widow Reed's window! He placed the book on the table in front of Felicity and then waited, smiling, for Felicity's reaction.

Nan and William both let out delighted cries. Felicity only blinked and then stared at the book in disbelief. It was too beautiful for words. The leather on the cover was a deep, lustrous brown, and the shiny gilt along its edges and on the title glistened in the candle-light.

Father's face clouded. "Are you not pleased, daughter?"

Felicity gave a sigh of pleasure. "Oh yes, Father," she said, "but I thought the book had been sold long ago. It disappeared from Widow Reed's window . . ."

Father grinned. "The book *had* been sold— to me. As soon as I returned from Portsmouth, I went by Widow Reed's shop and purchased it for you."

"Widow Reed never let on," Felicity said.

"It would have spoiled the surprise," Mother said, beaming.

Felicity hugged the book to her chest. "Oh, Father, Mother, thank you! 'Tis a wonderful gift!"

Father's answer was quiet, and his eyes shone with emotion. "It is your mother and I who are grateful, dear Lissie, for the gift we were given eleven years ago when you were born—and the gift you've continually given to us ever since, just by being you."

Felicity's throat closed up so that she couldn't answer. Suddenly tears were sliding down her cheeks, and she didn't know why.

She hadn't been so happy in a very long time. At that moment Rose brought in dessert— luscious apple cobbler with a smooth sweet sauce—and everyone's attention was drawn away from Felicity to exclaiming over the treat, and to eating.

Then the clink of silverware and china resumed, and Ben and Father began to talk about the store: what supplies were low, what needed to be ordered to replenish stock. Mother was fussing at William for gulping his milk and eating too fast and at Nan for talking with her mouth full. *Everything is back to normal,* thought Felicity.

She looked around her and tried to fasten it all in her memory just as it was: the faces of her family gathered at the table, the chatter of their voices, the flickering candlelight and the sweet smell of melting wax, the sleepy noises of Polly in her cradle, the sharp scent of pine logs burning on the hearth. How familiar it all was, and how dear to her.

How often had she taken for granted that

everyone she loved would be near and that everything safe and secure and warm would go on just as it always had? No more, she decided. No more.

Felicity smiled. Her family had forgotten about her, it seemed. Or at least they had forgotten Felicity the Hero. Now she was just plain Felicity Merriman again. And that was the way she liked it.

She picked up her spoon and scooped up a huge bite of apple cobbler.

LOOKING BACK

A PEEK INTO THE PAST

Patriot and British soldiers fighting in Massachusetts in 1775

In the spring of 1776, tensions between Patriots and Loyalists were growing worse. Patriots, like Felicity's family, wanted the American colonies to be free from British rule. Loyalists, like Elizabeth's family, thought that the colonies should remain loyal to the king of England. Fighting had already begun between the British and Patriot armies, and everyone knew the conflict would soon explode into war.

A year and a half before Felicity's story starts, Patriot leaders had gathered in Philadelphia for the First Continental Congress.

Patriot leaders at the First Continental Congress

Angry about the high taxes that the king was charging on goods shipped from England, the Continental Congress decided that the American colonies should fight back by refusing to trade with England. Beginning in 1775, colonists were supposed to *boycott*, or refuse to buy or sell, English goods.

The Continental Congress knew that the boycott would cause hardships for colonists. Families relied on products from England—everything from tea to cloth, sugar, and salt—and now they would have to find ways to make do without them. Storekeepers would suffer even more, since they could no longer sell the English goods that had always filled their shops. On top of that, many colonists did not support the Patriots or the boycott.

To support the boycott, colonial women learned to make their own thread and cloth.

So the Continental Congress looked for a way to make the boycott stick. They decided that every

A shop in Colonial Williamsburg

county in the colonies should elect a Committee of Safety to make sure that people obeyed the boycott. Anyone who didn't would be punished as an enemy of the Patriot cause.

The Committees of Safety quickly became very powerful—and very successful. Within a year, the once-busy trade between England and the American colonies had almost stopped.

Angered by the boycott, England sent warships to the colonies instead of trading ships.

The frightening events that happen to Mr. McLeod and Mr. Merriman in the story show how Committees of Safety operated.

A person suspected of breaking the boycott or hurting the Patriot cause in other ways would be called before the committee. His business records could be taken and inspected, as Mr. Merriman's ledger was. Storekeepers were especially likely to be accused, since they did most of the buying and selling in the colonies.

Committees often published the names of the accused in the newspapers. The publicity could

Newspapers printed the names of storekeepers who continued to sell British goods.

cause lasting damage to a person's reputation and business. Committees of Safety could also fine people, take their goods and auction them, and even order suspected Loyalists to leave the colony.

Mob violence was a real danger for people accused by a Committee of Safety, because angry Patriots saw them as enemies on the wrong side of the brewing war.

As the colonists chose sides in the war, neighbor turned against neighbor. Patriot mobs beat Loyalists or poured hot tar on them—a horribly painful process that could cause burns, scars, and even death. Loyalists carried out equally cruel acts against Patriots.

Patriot mobs brutally tarred and feathered Loyalist men and forced British tea down their throats.

In places where many Scottish immigrants settled, such as North Carolina and Virginia, Scots were often special targets of Patriot violence. Prejudice against the Scottish grew worse as large numbers of Scots joined the Loyalist side. Eventually, life in the colonies became so difficult for Scottish immigrants that tens of

A Loyalist family fleeing to safety in Canada

thousands left. Many slipped away in secret, leaving their homes and possessions behind, just as Fiona's family does.

Patriots and Loyalists had at least one thing in common during these dangerous times, however—they were all eager for news. Newspapers were widely read, and important towns like Williamsburg had several weekly newspapers.

Widow Reed is fictional, but a woman named

This newspaper was printed by Williamsburg publisher Clementina Rind in 1774. Several colonial newspapers were published by women.

Clementina Rind did publish Williamsburg's *Virginia Gazette* in 1773 and 1774. Women published several other major newspapers during Felicity's time, too.

Shortly after Felicity's mystery ends, newspapers printed one of the biggest stories in American history—the signing of the Declaration of Independence on July 4, 1776. Six years of war would follow, however, before Patriots and Loyalists finally put down their arms and began to build a new nation together in peace.

George Washington's soldiers raise the American flag at war's end.

ABOUT THE AUTHOR

 Elizabeth McDavid Jones has lived most of her life in North Carolina. Her earliest passions were animals and writing. As a girl, she especially loved to write stories about animals.

Today, she lives in Virginia with her husband and children. She is the author of another Felicity mystery, *Peril at King's Creek.* She also wrote five American Girl History Mysteries: *The Night Flyers,* which won the 2000 Edgar Allan Poe Award for Best Children's Mystery; *Secrets on 26th Street; Watcher in the Piney Woods; Mystery on Skull Island;* and *Ghost Light on Graveyard Shoal,* a 2004 Agatha Award nominee for Best Children's/Young Adult Mystery.